THE WHITE REVIEW

23

T0152148

The Uses of Queer Art KEVIN BRAZIL 15

Interview MARGO JEFFERSON 26

Art ALLISON KATZ 33

The Great Awake JULIA ARMFIELD 49

Poetry REBECCA GOSS 61

Faces in a Face LINA MERUANE *tr.* ANDREA ROSENBERG 65

Interview ANNIE ERNAUX 74

Poetry IMOGEN CASSELS 81

Art BETTINA SAMSON 87

Fragments NANAE AOYAMA *tr.* POLLY BARTON 99

Poetry A. K. BLAKEMORE 117

Interview MERNET LARSEN 122

All the Right Moves SANDIP KURIAKOSE 147

Roundtable ON CLASS 156

Wisteria OLGA TOKARCZUK

tr. ANTONIA LLOYD-JONES 167

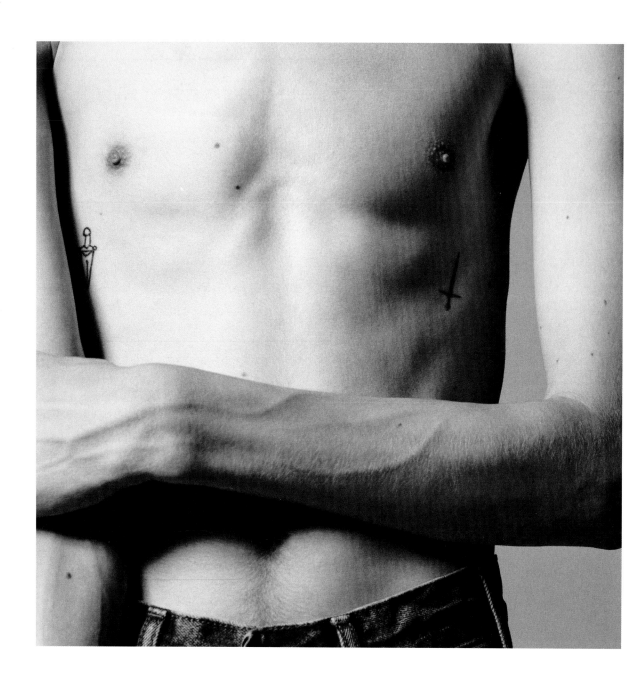

CELINE

MICHAEL LANDY
SCALED-DOWN

2 OCTOBER - 17 NOVEMBER 2018

THOMAS DANE GALLERY
3 Duke Street, St James's London, SW1
www.thomasdanegallery.com

Francesca Woodman
Italian Works

Victoria Miro VENICE

IL CAPRICORNO · SAN MARCO 1994
30124 VENICE · ITALY

15 SEPTEMBER – 15 DECEMBER 2018

GODAI SAHARA

Gao Gallery
26 September - 27 October 2018

MATTHEW PEERS

Sunday Art Fair
4 October - 7 October 2018

GAO

www.gao.gallery
unit 7, 88 mile end road, london e1 4un

Michele Abeles
Framing a Match

Sadie Coles   HQ

01 November – 15 December 2018
Tuesday–Saturday 11–6

Sadie Coles HQ
62 Kingly Street London W1B 5QN

www.sadiecoles.com

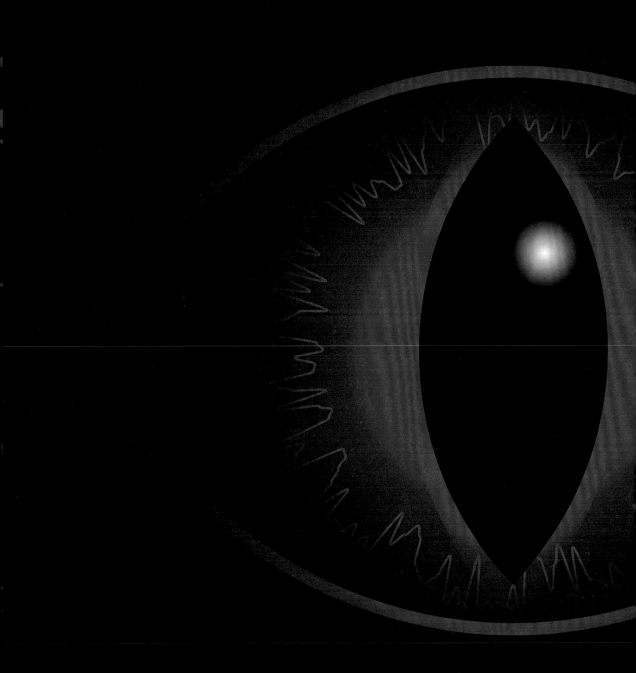

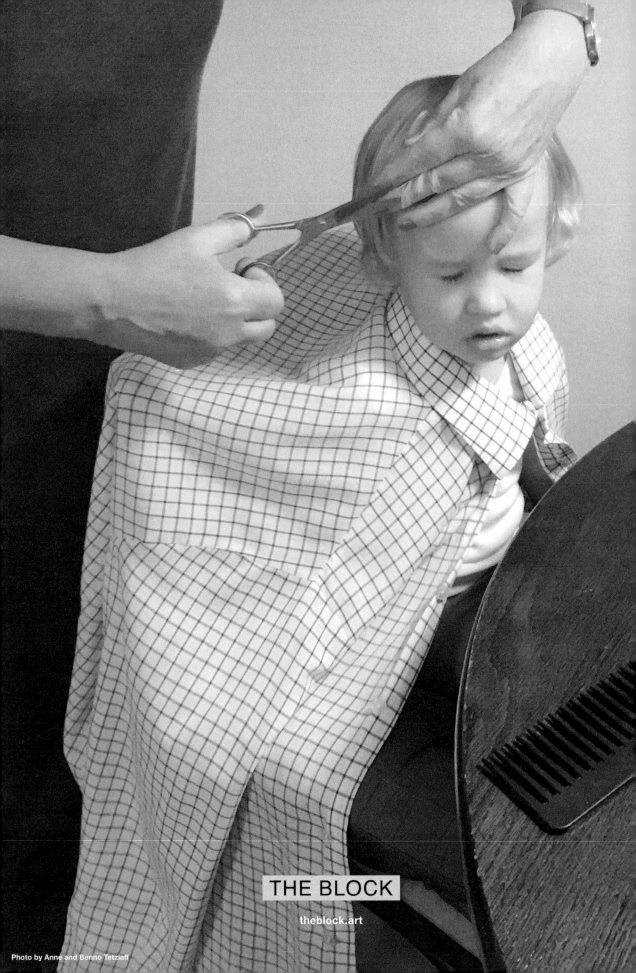

THE BLOCK

theblock.art

TULARE: Scenes from California's Central Valley   Jake Longstreth

ISBN 978-0-9992655-2-9 / THE ICE PLANT

Parasol unit
foundation for contemporary art

FREE ADMISSION
14 Wharf Road
London N1 7RW
parasol-unit.org

Heidi Bucher
19 September – 9 December 2018

Kindly supported by:

ART MENTOR FOUNDATION LUCERNE

swiss arts council
pro helvetia

STANLEY THOMAS
JOHNSON
FOUNDATION

SWISS
cultural
fund UK

Hyon Gyon
23 January – 31 March 2019

Kindly supported by:

Rachel Maclean
20 Sept–16 Dec 2018

**ZABLUDOWICZ
COLLECTION**

Free Entry
Thursday to Sunday 12–6pm
176 Prince of Wales Road
London NW5 3PT
zabludowiczcollection.com

Published by The White Review, October 2018
Edition of 1,800

Printed by Unicum, Tilburg
Typeset in Nouveau Blanche

ISBN No. 978-0-9957437-5-5

The White Review is a registered charity (number 1148690)

The White Review, 243 Knightsbridge, London SW7 1DN
www.thewhitereview.org

EDITORIAL

Issues of *The White Review* are not planned around a theme, but sometimes one asserts itself. Speaking to the writer Margo Jefferson, Zinzi Clemmons suggests we might think of Jefferson's work as 'arguing for nuance in order to rethink identity'. With contributors from across a wide range of experiences and nationalities (we count eight), this issue argues for the importance of a multiplicity of voices, and the opportunity for those voices to contradict and complicate themselves over time. In their own ways, each contributor measures the distance between their origins and the way they consider their identities today, and interrogates the idea of identity as a fixed or single state.

'I wanted to find a place for myself,' explains Jefferson. 'I didn't want to come up with performances of what I was calculating and sometimes seeing as the preferred authentic stances. So I had to find a legitimate space.' Annie Ernaux, in her interview with long-term fan Lauren Elkin, traces the gap between her working-class origins and her current status as one of France's pre-eminent writers: 'It's very spatial, as if there were two different places that had to be brought together: the place I started from, which has a certain violence, and the world of literature. In a way, every time I write, I'm conquering something.' This difference Ernaux identifies, which is the continued difficulty of accessing culture if you are from a working-class or minority background, is something we wanted to recognise through our roundtable on class. Participants share the ways they came into consciousness about their own class identities, the compassion required to approach our differences, and the limits of diversity measures. It's a subject far too complex and difficult for a single session to do it justice; over the coming months we'll continue the conversation on our website.

Elsewhere, we present a wide-ranging interview with the artist Mernet Larsen, who explains the way she began to refigure her earlier work to find new stories and meanings within it, resisting the idea of the finished artwork or any single interpretation. Allison Katz, too, repeatedly samples and adapts her own images, and we're excited to have an original piece by her as our front cover, followed by a series of her highly playful posters. Kevin Brazil considers what a queer museum might look like – one which recognises selfhood as an invention, and challenges the impulse to contain and tame an identity that is by its nature unfixed. Sandip Kuriakose applies similar thinking to the art and gay scenes in Delhi, two worlds united by the centrality of images, through which identities – and desires – are constructed. In an essay exploring her Palestinian-Chilean ancestry, Lina Meruane asks how faces can reveal, hide or deceive. As she narrates a trip to Beit Jala to visit relatives, she examines the shifting sands of history and memory.

We're delighted to publish the first English translation of Japanese author Nanae Aoyama; 'Kakera' (published here as 'Fragments') made her in 2009 the youngest ever winner of Japan's prestigious Kawabata Yasunari Prize. We're also thrilled to present newly translated fiction from 2018's Man Booker International Prize winner Olga Tokarczuk, a deliciously dark and surreal story of unusual familial relations. Finally, we are excited to publish 'The Great Awake' by Julia Armfield, the winner of our fifth annual short story prize. Praised by the judges for its ambitious concept, and the skill with which Armfield pulls it off, the story is testament to the continued power of the prize to discover and create a space for new talent.

In June 2018 a crowd assembled in Tate Britain to ask: 'What does a queer museum look like?' Surrounded by the airless eroticism of Pre-Raphaelite portraiture, all drowning Ophelias and hieratic Lady Macbeths, the founder of the Museum of Transology, E-J Scott, asked a mixture of queer activists and members of the public how to go about building a museum in which 'we can save the queer past for the queer future' and where 'we all can become curators of queer heritage'. For some, a queer museum was necessary so the world could see that queers exist. For others, a separate queer museum would only absolve other institutions from diversifying their collections. One speaker questioned why black queerness should be defined by a museum, itself a European institution long bound up with the colonial subjugation of Africa and its diaspora. There was little threat of the discussion getting out of hand among the Tate's polite, predominately white middle-class audience. But just in case, Scott had distributed oversized plastic toy tools among queer activists in the audience, to control the order of the discussion. One by one they were called in: hammer, screwdriver, spanner. Building a queer museum, it was suggested, was a matter of finding 'the right tools for the job'.

A museum is an institution for relating things in time. It arranges objects not just in rooms, but in a history that moves in a continuous line from past to present, in order to show the development of a communal identity. In theory this can be the universal humanity disingenuously imagined by the British Museum or the Louvre; in practice it is often the more narrowly defined ethnic nation produced by Tate Britain, whose natural continuity and organic reproduction across time is enabled by the museum's presentation of an archive of 'our' past. Perhaps one reason why the discussion at the Tate had to be handled so delicately, as if disagreement was something that only happened among children, was because of a suspicion that as a way of using time a museum is inherently contradictory with the idea of queerness, at least as it has so far been understood: queerness as that which is opposed to what is 'natural', that which believes that genders and sexualities change across time and place, that which accepts the very idea that we have a 'gender' and 'sexuality' as historically novel, and really very strange, ways of understanding the self.

It may be that queer is simply what you make it, and that people might want a museum of queer art and history. And why not? No one should be begrudged the comfort of seeing themselves in the art of the past, so long as they recognise that it comes at the cost of fixing a particular way of using that past — as a resource for the definition of a communal identity in the present. The very real anger that accompanies debates about what belongs in a museum, queer or otherwise, shows that the conflict about who and what goes in a museum is a conflict about who and what we are. The fact that these debates seem so intractable is that co-opting the past to create any identity inevitably winds up in an endgame of definitions: my definition, your definition; my museum, your museum. But there are other ways of using the history, ways that don't see it as something to be used: that see the past, for better or worse, as not really useful at all.

*

In 1992, Hamad Butt suspended nine sealed glass spheres containing chlorine gas from the centre of the roof of the John Hansard Gallery in Southampton. The spheres hung together in groups of three, like snapshots from the swing of a pendulum, creating the illusion of movement and a sense that the glass might shatter at any moment and release the toxic gas within. In one corner of the triangular gallery, three pointed glass tubes containing bromine gas were placed on top of metal poles that curved outwards and inwards as they ascended from the ground, the sharpened tips of a clenching claw. On the opposite gallery wall were installed ladders whose rungs were glass cylinders containing iodine in a vacuum and an infra-red heating unit. A timer turned the heating unit on and off so that the iodine transformed back and forth from gas to solid.

At room temperature, chlorine is an extremely reactive pale green gas. If inhaled, it combines with water to produce hydrochloric acid and release nitric oxides, so that the acid and oxides dissolve the lungs from within. Bromine appears at room temperature as a dark red liquid that evaporates into a gas of the same bloody colour. It does not produce an immediately visible reaction upon contact with human skin, and this delay makes it all the more dangerous. Inadvertently the entire body can be exposed to damage, the skin later erupting with blisters and ulcers. Iodine is a lustrous violet solid that when heated transforms directly from a solid to a gas: a process known as sublimation. Although contact with skin in its pure state can produce irritation, iodine plays a prominent role in human medicine as it is a powerful disinfectant — it cures by killing.

These three chemical sculptures — *Cradle, Hypostasis*, and *Substance Sublimation Unit* — made up an installation called *Familiars*, Butt's first commissioned solo exhibition. Born in Lahore, Pakistan, in 1962, Butt grew up in Britain and studied chemistry and physics, later graduating with a degree in Fine Art from Goldsmiths in 1990. He entered Goldsmiths mythology by receiving one of the highest marks ever awarded for his final year project, *Transmission*, an installation consisting of a vitrine containing maggots and sugar solution, surrounded by glass books emitting ultraviolet light, so that the birth, life, and death of the flies could only be viewed through filtered glasses. Stephen Foster, the director of the Hansard Gallery, commissioned *Familiars* after seeing *Transmission* at Butt's graduation show. Like the tutors at Goldsmiths, Foster thought Butt was a 'genius', albeit a shy and quiet one, and that *Transmission* depicted a darkly ironic view of life and death: 'People are attracted to things that destroy them.' Both *Transmission* and *Familiars* confront us with the danger of our desire: we crave the sugar that kills us, we heal with chemicals that poison us. Both installations ask us, too, what we desire of art: what do we want to use it to do?

Transmission was later shown at Milch Gallery, which was founded in 1990, and which became a meeting point between London's underground queer scene and the generation of artists then graduating from Goldsmiths who would later be marketed as the Young British Artists. Butt's work was followed there by the strikingly similar installation which first brought Damien Hirst fame: *In and Out of Love* (1991), in which butterfly pupae attached to canvas hatched, lived, and died over the course of an exhibition. Ros Carter, a curator at the Hansard who helped install *Familiars*, recalls the 'extremity of elements within the gay scene' centred around Milch. It was the height of the AIDS crisis, the style was 'overt and aggressive, with connections to S&M subculture'. There was 'a general culture of risk-taking and doing things to your body' that the art world shared not only with the queer underground, but also with the club scene which by the early 1990s was flooded by drugs. 'There seemed to be a lot of chemicals going around,' says Carter, 'and a general air of toxicity.' Carter, however, was certain that Butt didn't take part in the hedonism. He was 'a gentle soul, measured, reserved'.

In the texts written whilst creating *Familiars*, Butt wrote of his desire to explore what he called 'apprehensions': the 'seizure and arresting of perceptions' which we 'anticipate by fear to the point of understanding'. Apprehensions come after the biochemical processes corresponding to anxiety or stress. Fear and unease, Butt wrote, are 'understood, made comfortable, apprehended by the language that takes hold of this quality of experience'. He wanted to convey the apprehensions caused by the spread of AIDS — 'We cannot respond to this epidemic without fear and confusion, without aching to know why' — but knew that for the artist to 'legislate, so to speak, for the order of apprehending AIDS and the fear of AIDS... enjoins one to ironise the privileged role of the eye'. These apprehensions, at once so intangible and so consequential to those who acquire HIV, cannot be shown in a picture or described in writing. They are something more diffuse: a sense of poison in the air, of latent toxicity in the atmosphere, of fragile protection giving way.

A year after Butt died of AIDS-related illness in 1994, *Familiars* was exhibited at the Tate in the group exhibition *Rites of Passage* (1995). Foster, who Butt had asked to publish his writings posthumously, remembers how for years the Tate refused to acquire *Familiars* for its permanent collection when it was offered to them by Butt's brother Jamal. Foster is certain that this wasn't due to institutional homophobia; rather, it came from a worry about 'how to preserve the toxic chemicals'. Museums preserve objects, not atmospheres; things, not terrors. Butt, he remembers, took the risk less seriously: he used to sleep with the glass vessels under his bed. After he died, Jamal stored them in the attic of his house in North Finchley. Eventually, after years of campaigning by Jamal Butt, Diego Ferrari, Jean Fisher and others, the Tate acquired *Familiars* for its permanent collection in 2015, although it has never been publicly exhibited.

In September 2018 the same samples of chlorine, iodine and bromine that Butt sealed in glass in 1992 were taken out of storage and *Familiars* re-installed in the Hansard's new building in Southampton. Foster, who recently retired as the gallery's director, is curating an exhibition called *Time After Time* that recreates a number of installations he has commissioned over the past thirty years, with *Familiars* appearing alongside work by John Latham, Caroline Bergvall, Charlotte Posenenske, Walter van Rijn and Victor Burgin. The aim of the exhibition is to explore the curatorial issues involved in translating sculptural installations across time and place. Or as Carter, now Senior Curator at the Hansard, puts it: 'Some things are made to be ephemeral, and you have to be careful not to re-stage things for the sake of it. If something is tied to a particular moment there is a reason for that, and you have to be careful not to be self-indulgent, or to do it out of nostalgia.' Just as there is a tension between desire and danger at the heart of Butt's work, so too there is a tension in every act of curatorial reconstruction between the urge to do justice to a forgotten work and a cheap nostalgia that would betray it.

Hamad Butt might seem to be precisely the kind of artist, long neglected by official art installations, whose work is now ripe to be recuperated within a queer art historical museum. As his story shows, of course, such artists are never actually forgotten. They have always been remembered by curators, critics and other artists who have worked to achieve the mundane but consequential steps that, over time, lead to an artist's work enduring: publications, catalogues, purchases by national collections. Yet any attempt to use his work to build a narrative of queer art history – to use it to create an identity – is complicated by that work's own attitude to its use. The desire to use the past in a museum cannot overlook the fact that works from the past might take a rather ironic view of being used in the future.

Familiars doesn't just play with the expectation that art made by a queer person with HIV should be useful – a document of suffering recorded for the future. It also exaggerates its own use of these chemicals as a device to convey the atmosphere of fear surrounding AIDS in the early nineties. The pendulums only offer the illusion of movement, the glass claw only appears to clench. Foster remembers that Butt loved the fact that the Hansard provided gas masks and asbestos suits alongside the installation, even though they probably weren't necessary. Butt's writings show a deeper play with the idea that *Familiars* was being used to convey the fear of AIDS. He notes that Susan Sontag's analysis of 1950s sci-fi movies showed that visions of apocalyptic destruction caused by fear of infection actually involve 'imaginative complicity with disaster': 'The trauma of the body to which fantasy inures us, is the opposition to collective nightmares that inspire a sense of humour.' To believe that a threat can damage you to the point of trauma is what gives that threat its power, and it is what forecloses other forms of resistance. Butt asked that the book containing these notes be accompanied by a hologram of the Bollywood actress Meena Kumari dancing in a scene from the film *Pakeezah* (1972). Kumari is one of the great camp icons of Bollywood, and in *Pakeezah* she plays the role which distills the reason so many Indian gay men identified with her: a courtesan who hides her endless self-sacrifice in love behind a mask of decorum, and who can only acknowledge her suffering by transforming it into an exaggerated melodrama of song and dance. Ever so subtly, Butt's writings camp the idea of art being used to convey the trauma of AIDS. *Familiars* takes unseriously the belief that art should be used to provide a historical document of queer suffering or identity, and sends a message to its future viewers asking why we might want it to do so.

*

If we don't yet know what a queer museum looks like, museums and galleries around the world are constantly seeking and discovering the art which would go inside it. In 2017 MOCA Los Angeles presented *Axis Mundo: Queer Networks in Chicano LA*, the first major retrospective of queer Chicanx artists, stretching back to videos of the 1970s guerilla drag performances of Edmundo 'Mundo' Meza and Robert 'Cyclona' Legoretta. That same year the Museum of Contemporary Art Taipei became the first major institution in Asia to host an exhibition of LGBTQ Asian art, with its show *Spectrosynthesis*. Although its focus was mostly on contemporary work, the exhibition reached back to include Shiy De-Jinn's 1960s portraits of androgynous youths and Tseng Kwong Chi's *East Meets West* series of self-portraits (1979–89), anchoring the work of present artists within a narrative of queer Asian art history. Peter Hujar, whose composed monochrome portraits of Susan Sontag, Candy Darling and Robert Mapplethorpe have shaped a romanticised image of downtown New York in the era before AIDS, has been the subject of recent retrospectives in Spain, the Netherlands and New York. Hujar's *Orgasmic Man* (1969), a photograph of a man's face twisted in the pleasurable agony of orgasm, provided the cover of Hanya Yanagihara's bestselling *A Little Life* (2015), positioning the novel's melodramatic saga of queer suffering, as if to validate it, in a distinctively queer history of intertwined pleasure and pain.

Even a show focused on contemporary art's preoccupation with gender and sexuality, 2017's *Trigger: Gender as a Tool and a Weapon* at the New Museum, New York, saw artists like Josh Faught, Ellen Lesperance and Candice Lin preoccupied with archives of the queer past. Reina Gossett and Sasha Wortzel's *Lost in the Music* (2017) included Gossett's now rare footage of the black trans activist Marsha P. Johnson; the question of who owns this footage is at the centre of a bitter battle between Gossett and the producers of the 2016 Netflix documentary *The Death and Life of Marsha P. Johnson*. Archives of queer history have been valuable commodities. Valuable, and value-adding: the first exhibition shown at Peckham Levels, a redevelopment 'bringing new life' (think Poké bowls, rented workspaces, Instagrammable interiors) to one of London's major historically black communities, was *Southwark QueerStory* (2018), a celebration of the borough's queer history, promoted with a photograph from the 1980s of a kissing black and white lesbian couple. This area of London has less positive histories of race relations, such as those told by the poet Jay Bernard in their recent poem-sequence *Surge*: the 1981 New Cross fire in which thirteen black people died, and which prompted mass demonstrations against the failure of the predominately white police to investigate the disaster. But evidently, these don't go as well with 'redevelopment' as images which instrumentalise queer love as the solution to racial domination.

The desire for a queer archive has even seeped into the practice of living queer artists. In an interview about her photographic portraits of black lesbians living in South Africa, Zanele Muholi has explained that 'I have created an archive that never existed in this country before.' For Muholi, if an archive of black lesbian life doesn't exist, it has to be invented: an identity can't be imagined without the contents of a museum. Karol Radziszewski, founder of the first Polish queer art magazine, *DIK Fagazine*, created the virtual *Queer Archive Institute* to host his collection of interviews, oral histories and magazines documenting queer life in Eastern Europe during the Communist era. Radziszewski wanted to preserve this material so it can be used for future artistic projects: 'everything that contemporary queer artists are doing is becoming a queer archive'.

For other artists, a queer archive is important only insofar as it can be used to imagine a different future. Paul Maheke's *A fire for a public circle* (2018), shown at Chisenhale Gallery in London, presented a daily performance whose background was a mural depicting a comic-book vision of outer space, a childish cosmology of distant galaxies. Each afternoon Titilayo Adebayo and Heather Agyepong enacted a performance which re-staged movements from performances by Bruce Nauman, Felix Gonzalez-Torres, Eisa Jocson and Michael Jackson, whilst reciting texts by Audre Lorde and Judith Butler, among others. Maheke wanted these performances to rearticulate pre-existing material, 'to re-work it for the present moment': a process of 'queerness and blackness as modes of production'. Gestures were summoned from the past to create a 'space for reinvention' in order to 'think through identity outside of "identity politics"'. The particular archive summoned in each performance existed only to create something new in the moment, disappearing without being fixed into a purportedly authoritative canon.

For the Istanbul Queer Art Collective, founded by Onur Gökhan Gökçek, Seda Ergül and Tuna Erdem, performance and restaging are also central to queerness as a mode of production. Since 2012 they have enacted Fluxus performances in Turkey and elsewhere: performing the instructions left in the so-called 'event scores' composed by artists like John Cage and Yoko Ono. They do so in order to inhabit the perception, common in Turkey, that both contemporary art and queerness are Western imports. Erdem and Ergul explain that 'being a lesbian is often referred to as something we have "copied" from the West'. They want these restagings and the copying they enact to fail; not to 'fail better', like Beckett, so as to make use of failure – 'we just want to fail'. For Erdem and Ergul, queerness is an attitude to time: they want the failure of their restagings to produce 'transtemporal drag', to show what does not or should not translate across time. Their performances show the artifice of an assumed continuity between past and present, and between the West and its others, just as the point of drag is to show the artifice of natural masculinity and femininity, and to enjoy making it useless.

The discussion at Tate Britain imagining what a queer museum might look like was organised in the aftermath of *Queer British Art 1861-1967* (2017), an exhibition which offered the closest Britain has had to an official seal of approval for an archive of queer art history. Its wide historical range forced its curator, Clare Barlow, to confront an issue other exhibitions of queer art, more focused on the recent past, could evade. The exhibition presented work from times when, as Barlow wrote, 'the modern terminology of "lesbian", "gay", "bisexual" and "trans" was unrecognised'. Neither was 'queer', but this was absolved of responsibility to historical accuracy. 'Queer' named past sexual identities 'that don't map onto modern sexual identities': Victorian and Edwardian artists understood themselves as 'Uranian', 'inverts', or members of a 'third sex', but certainly not queer. And yet, 'queer' also named what these artists have in common with the contemporary notion of 'queer' as an oppositional sexual identity. The paradox of queerness naming something historically specific to the present as well as something continuous across time was shirked in the physical curation of the show, which moved in linear fashion, room by room, from the desires of the Victorian era to the explicit sadism of Francis Bacon in the 1960s. But this contradiction is not something that a different hanging could solve, or even that any museum could solve: it is a paradox latent in the very concept of queer itself.

*

The freedom of queerness hits like a revelation: it doesn't have to be this way because it hasn't always been this way. Sex, desire, my gender, my body: these were different in the past and therefore can be different in the present. Few things are more convincing when trying to prove there is nothing natural about dividing the human species into a hierarchy based on what they desire than being able to point, as Michel Foucault famously did in *The History of Sexuality* (1978), to the moment in history when homosexuality and heterosexuality were invented. The same move – using knowledge of the past to expose the myths of the present – frees you from believing that you are always only a man or a woman, that there are only things called men and women, that you will only ever desire one person, that desire is that important at all.

This leaves today's queers with a strange relationship to the past. The freedom of queerness is the realisation that the self and its desires are cultural, not natural: they change, and they have never been fixed. This means the queer can only know history in order to do without it, at least in any deep and extended sense. If selves and sexualities can be invented, then before a certain point they didn't exist. Queerness is perhaps the most modern identity of them all, accepting of the most intimate aspects of our lives that all that is solid melts into air, all that is holy is profaned. Queers are cut off from the past by the revelation that sets them free. Queers need to do without history in order to be queer.

Queerness, too, was invented, which is to say that activists, academics and artists have participated in a collective decision to make 'queer' a term of communal identification and recognition. The paradox of queerness's relationship to history was acknowledged at its moment of invention. In the early 1990s Judith Butler wrote that there was a tension at the heart of queer as the name for an identity, due to its being reappropriated from a shaming insult to a badge of pride. If, Butler wrote:

> the term "queer" is to be a site of collective contestation, the point of departure for a set of historical reflections and futural imaginings, it will have to remain that which is, in the present, never fully owned... This also means that it will doubtless have to be yielded in favour of terms that do that political work more effectively.

For Butler, at least in 1993, the potential of queer as a political concept lay not simply in the refusal to ascribe it a fixed definition – something true in a banal way of any identity – but in the willingness to eventually abolish itself in favour of other, ultimately more liberating ways of imagining selves and communities. If we remember that something is invented, we can imagine it ceasing to exist. The explosion of queer art and theory since the 1990s was animated, maybe even defined, by the tension between queerness as a means of looking back, and as a way to imagine the future. As queerness has expanded beyond labelling a sexual preference to naming lives and communities that are not governed by the progress from childhood to child-bearing, or by the dictates and bonds of biological reproduction, queerness has come, for many, to be nothing so much as a way of living time.

What kind of time is produced by an archive, a heritage, a museum? Part of Butler's hesitation about embracing queerness as a political identity came from the knowledge that, in the United States at least, earlier sexual identities like 'gay' and 'lesbian' gained political rights and cultural recognition only insofar as they modelled themselves on the ethnic identities of the Civil Rights era: blackness, Asian-American, Chicanx. Queer held out the promise of a different form of identity than 'gay' or 'lesbian': one which wouldn't be modelled on an ethnicity and would only use the past to imagine a different future – one in which queerness might cease to exist. Ethnic identities deserve civil and political rights because, or so the story goes, they name distinct cultures and ways of life and the preservation of cultures is a good in itself. Nothing shows the distinction of a culture – and thus its worth – more than the fact that it has existed over time, and that there is a constantly renewing continuity between past and present. In an ethnicity, culture transforms back into nature, as the eighteenth-century German philosopher Johann Gottfried Herder – one founder of the concept of ethnicity – imagined: 'the earth might be regarded as a garden, where here the one and there the other human national plant flowered in keeping with its own formation and nature'. National museums and archives are built to show the continuity of the natural species across history, which persists in a time modelled on biological reproduction. The first modern museums were museums of natural history; the art museums of today make each work of art the product of a natural species, bonded across time by the biological reproduction that queerness tries to escape.

It might be that the desire for a queer museum is just one moment in an oscillation between the idea of queerness being used to reflect upon the past and to imagine the future. But it also might be true that, at least in the art world, the temporal tension at the heart of queerness has finally dissipated: it is no longer willing to admit the artifice of queer as a sexual identity to the point of imagining its disappearance. Maybe enough artists, curators, museums and viewers have decided that queers need the same kind of heritage as every other ethnic group in a liberal capitalist democracy. Maybe they have realised that liberal capitalist democracies find it easier to grant rights to cultures than to redistribute wealth to classes. Maybe the thrill of knowing your identity is made-up has come to feel hollow when faced with the comforts of imagining your reflection in the past.

There is nothing inherently revolutionary about novelty. The proclamation of being without precedent sounds a lot like the slogan of a new product for the market. History can tell us some important truths. People suffered in the past for desires, touches and glances that today seem so casual you forget how much they mean. People suffer today for the same reasons, and there is something obscene about the fact that millions are dying of AIDS in Africa and Asia whilst posters appear in London and New York instructing you in the joys of being untransmissable with the help of one pill a day. But if the past is only being used to tell others who you are, it's unclear whether it is really being remembered at all.

In 1952 Jean Genet wrote to Jean-Paul Sartre: 'In any event the significance of homosexuality is this: A refusal to continue the world. Then, to alter sexuality. The child or the adolescent who refuses the world and turns towards his own sex, knowing himself that he is a man, in struggling against this useless manliness is going to try to dissolve it.'

For Genet, homosexuality doesn't have to only replace a natural order with its cultural reality: it can also just make the natural useless, and enjoy doing so too. Its emblems were the flowers he imagined that bloomed from being spat upon, that wreathed his drag queen Divine: artificial flowers, not the living roses of nature. The idea that a sexuality is not a definition you identify with, but a way of taking pleasure in being useless, is neither specific to Genet nor to the identity of a 'homosexual'. It is what drives the spectacle drag kings make of the masculinity normally used to subjugate women; it is what enables the pleasure of camp, which delights in what is outdated; it is what marks any person whose desires aren't tied to reproduction: from the point of view of evolution they are simply useless. Queerness as a practice, rather than identity, can be a way of being useless, of enjoying making things useless, of not needing to use. It can be a way of doing without the things you find yourself born into, since for all that queers might want to refuse to continue the world through reproduction, none of us can escape being born.

*

The attraction of a museum is that it holds an archive of the past, ensuring that what could be forgotten will be remembered. But it also turns the past into a resource to be mined – with the right tools for the job – to create an identity in the present. To do this requires a particular model of time, in which the present is organically reproduced from the past, like seeds from a flower. In 2018 it was announced that London will get its own queer museum, and in time other cities around the world will too, producing an international archive of what it means to be queer.

Just as the museum spread from Europe to the rest of the world, so too a certain archive of queerness will probably spread to Taipei, Mexico, and Johannesburg: drag, vogueing and dykes, but not hijra, mashoga or two-spirit. Different ways of using the past will continue to exist, ways that make useless notions of continuity modelled on nature; they might continue to be recognised as queer, or they might lead to other political practices and collectivities.

A museum of queer art would ensure that the past will not be forgotten, but we should never assume it is the only way of using time. Nor should we ever assume that it makes the past familiar. We call things familiar when we think we know them well, as if they are members of our family. The word assumes that we are most at home with the people who made us, that we are most comfortable with what is natural, with what we know how to use. Familiars are also the animals that assist practitioners of magic. They appear only to enable the essence of magical thinking: that pretending makes it true. We shouldn't forget, as Butt wrote of his *Familiars*, that one thing art can do is make the past disappear: 'There is the acknowledgement of loss and the numbness of its repetition, which moves us in particular to displace fear with some kind of charming dialogue; an ungraspable sleight of hand.'

MARGO JEFFERSON   INTERVIEW

I've had the privilege of knowing Margo Jefferson since 2011, when I took her class, The Critic as Artist, as a student in Columbia's graduate writing programme. I'd thought I knew all there was to know about Walter Benjamin, until she had us read *Berlin Childhood around 1900*, where I was introduced to the idea that a writer's life was worthy of detailed study; that it can illuminate their work when placed alongside it. It was to my great surprise and delight when, in her 2015 memoir *Negroland*, Jefferson placed her own life — a childhood in Chicago's black elite and an accomplished adulthood in journalism (she won the Pulitzer Prize for criticism in 1995) — under the scan of her unrelenting eye. When it was published, I had been out of grad school a couple of years, had moved away and hadn't seen her for as long, though I had already torn through her first book, *On Michael Jackson*, after reading everything of hers I could find online. Reading *Negroland* was like opening a portal into her mind, and just like Benjamin's *Berlin Childhood*, it offered new insights into a thinker I thought I already knew. It also taught me something about myself as a woman and a writer. I was so excited by it that I couldn't wait until I'd finished reading to tell her how much I loved it. 'It makes sense,' I wrote to her in an email, 'that in your memoir you would act as a critic — as black women, we are constantly forced to see ourselves through others' eyes, and thus become critics of our own lives. This is something I have always felt on some level, but confronted it in your book as plain truth.' Jefferson's work has not only challenged me to think about works of art more deeply, but to do the same in regards to my own life. For that, I, and her many readers, will always be grateful.   ZINZI CLEMMONS

TWR   A lot of your work investigates unexplored aspects of various identities, but primarily of race and gender. I might describe your project as arguing for nuance in order to rethink identity. You did it in *On Michael Jackson*, by connecting the dots of his personality and drawing attention to our blind spots about his persona. And you filled in a picture of black womanhood in *Negroland* by talking about privilege and vulnerability. In your essay about Nella Larsen ['On Writers and Writing; Authentic American', published in the *New York Times* in 2001] this is something that you say explicitly: that we need to abandon old notions of authenticity in regards to race, in regards to craft, and also in regards to how we think of people. There's a quote in *Negroland* that comes amidst a section where you discuss suicide: 'I found literary idols in Adrienne Kennedy, Nella Larsen, and Ntozake Shange, writers who'd dared to locate a sanctioned, forbidden space between white vulnerability and black invincibility.' Is this a conscious part of your project, or is it something that filters in unconsciously from your lived experience?
MJ   I think it's both. When I was starting out it was probably instinctual. I thought of myself as a progressive black feminist, so that meant I had a class analysis, a race analysis, and a gender analysis. But these particulars about identity and what's authentic and what's not — I followed my instincts with those. I began to think about them partly because they were enormously interesting to me, and some of that was autobiographical. I had grown up intellectually, socially, and also emotionally, in these spaces that bordered on neighbourhoods of various identities. That family down the block could be completely different. So I had to keep trying to make analytic and emotional sense of that, and if I didn't keep analysing it, then a couple of things could have happened. One, I could have gotten very class defensive about it, which was the last thing I was interested in doing — shifting into black respectability, into a conservative stance. That seems an unlikely position for me to have been tempted by, but criticism always tempts you towards certain kinds of lofty stances. The other thing, which is almost its opposite, is that I wanted to find a place for myself. I did not want to pretend to be, you know, more 'street' in origin than I was — I didn't want to come up with performances of what I was calculating and sometimes seeing as the preferred authentic stances. So I had to find a legitimate space. And I had to find allies, of course,

in that space. I was once having a conversation with Adrienne Kennedy about this, and we agreed that both of us, in our work, wanted to find a fixed space for black culture — and our culture, which was mixed within that — at the centre of white culture. That was our quest.

TWR   You've used the term 'cultural mulatto' in your criticism, and it's been used to describe you as well. The term 'mulatto' itself isn't used much today, but I think 'cultural mulatto' is still very much present. Do you still see that concept showing up today, and where do you see that conversation that you started with Adrienne Kennedy now?
MJ   The term is tricky, so let's instead think about concept, because it doesn't work in every context. You can't use a word like 'mulatto', or 'coloured', or 'Negro' without surrounding it with explications and qualifications that make very clear that you are stripping it of certain things and supplying it with certain others. You're revising it and renovating it. I would say that intersectionality is in many ways a more sophisticated take on — or an extension of — what we might call cultural mulatto-ism. I'm thinking particularly in culture and the arts. But one could say the same thing in terms of politics. There are so many kinds of mixed people now, people of colour who are mixed in various ways. We're just really beginning to quantify and analyse and emotionally dissect that. I think that's very, very fruitful. I encountered it a lot in England, with Caribbean blacks, with South Asians. Whenever I talked to Latinx critics, women in particular. Writers are continually probing and dramatising those states, and that move from what appears to be certainty to uncertainty. These identity changes, not in terms of tragedy, but negotiations. Code switching is a term I'm getting tired of, but code switching. And also understanding that that is a performance that's crucial to who you are. It's performance as a form of truth, not of lying. It's very tied to a different notion of authenticity which really now does include a sense of constructed, inherited identity that keeps reconstructing, and that you can negotiate and perform with. I mean, isn't that what we think of as identity these days? It doesn't mean it's any less deeply felt.

TWR   I think that, as time goes on, identity will increasingly be constituted performatively as we move away from biological links, in terms of gender and race and everything else. For example, because of our habits online, we're beginning to be defined much more by our interests, by the people we're friends with, and our politics.

MJ   And also, class was never biological, though it's been linked to biology. That's a huge factor as well that inflects every one of these mixtures.

TWR   In the 1977 documentary *Some American Feminists*, you gave a very good definition of what we would today define as intersectionality. I wonder how you engage with that theory? Also, I have a feeling that as a critic you might be resistant to labels such as intersectionality. What perhaps attracts you to that theory, and what might give you reservations about it?

MJ   In terms of what I've read of it, I'm really unreservedly attracted to intersectionality. It just seems, to me, to be a kind of theorisation or formalisation of all the things we've been talking about. It seems like a basic tool for understanding identities, and also clashes. If each of our intersectional structures could be visible, like architectural structures or movable sculptures, we would be able to see much more clearly. It would almost be like being able to read blueprints, or a doctor being able to read X-rays. But in terms of the language, have I used it much? I don't know that I have. In *Negroland*, I say race, class, gender, I call it my secular trinity. I was probably feeling, and that does address your language question, that where I was writing and in terms of the voice I was using, it would have sounded a little stilted, as if I was trying for a certain kind of intellectual properness. I don't think that would have to be the case in everything I write, by any means. It would depend on the essay and the subject. I try to be quite responsible, as a journalist and as a critic, to pay attention to more theoretical and scholarly materials, and I'm not against using them at all. But I just have to be very careful tonally with how they work in terms of my prose. So I don't want to seem to be showing off. I don't want to sound unduly laborious. It's just a negotiation for me.

TWR   Sometimes when we use rhetoric and terminology to stand in for ideas, they can be misused. And I wonder if, as a critic and someone with a sharp mind who is used to questioning, that might be part of why you've chosen not to use the term? In many ways, your entire body of work explains that term, it's almost redundant to use it.

MJ   That's very nice. You made a good point.

Rhetoric, including rhetoric that people you very much respect have all agreed on, jumps up and jumps out. It can alter the landscape of your prose and it can change the degrees in subtlety. As a critic, it can even change your position. It can also just get stale. There was a certain period when more general media critics and journalists got very excited about using 'deconstruct', and it started turning into a little winking cliche that was supposed to do the work for you.

TWR   Kimberlé Crenshaw introduced 'intersectionality' in a paper published in 1989, and it started to be used in the nineties, and I feel it's reached a saturation point today, almost thirty years later. But you're proof that its principles were widely held beforehand, and it's important to consider its history — or perhaps pre-history.

MJ   The work and words of black feminists came before its coining. What is black feminist analysis but a real documentation and insistence on the power and the place and the precedents of intersectionality? That was happening, and I was learning from it and taking from it, and also using my own words. That was the core strength of the black feminist analysis that was being worked on.

TWR   You consider yourself part of the women's movement?

MJ   Oh, absolutely.

TWR   I'm so eager to hear about your experience during that time.

MJ   I was actually just reading Reni Eddo-Lodge's book, *Why I'm No Longer Talking to White People About Race*, and I'm just starting the feminism chapter, where she says, kind of mournfully, that it hurts to call out racism among white feminists because feminism was actually my first entryway into really thinking hard about oppression. That was moving to me. That wasn't true for me because I grew up in the Civil Rights Movement. As we were getting out of college, my generation migrated to Black Power, along with the anti-war movement. My first exposure to feminism, which was almost entirely white feminism, was in 1969, when these little magazines started to come out. Flo Kennedy, Celestine Ware, Audre Lorde, Alice Walker and others insisted that we are absolute feminists. They said, you're doing white middle-class feminism, and that class thing was very important. And I was thrilled to read radicals like Ti-Grace Atkinson and Shulamith Firestone. I was able to connect with black feminists through a tiny little group I found in graduate school in 1971, and I went to some of their meetings and wrote about them, but we were kind of fugitives. But I never relinquished my feminist passion, and we women of colour started to find each other organisationally in the early seventies. The National Black Feminist Organisation started maybe a year later. A group of us, with June Jordan and Alice Walker, started a group that included lawyers, journalists, editors, critics, called The Sisterhood. We would meet maybe once a month, and I remember one woman wrote a letter saying, look, are we going to do political action or is this about handholding? Well, you know, it was very much about handholding, but also handholding as consciousness-raising, as emotional support, and also as a way of thinking about how black women artists and intellectuals could sustain themselves as a group and as individuals. And then there were black women scholars who really started putting that work on the map. This is all in the early and mid-seventies. By that time I had gone to *Newsweek*, and I wanted to write about everything that white male critics were not writing about. In our various places, we were creating a new and alternative canon. I was trying to cover that waterfront because the work was there, and all the artistic and activist communities around it were there. That felt very, very good, particularly because, in these mainstream publications, you could often feel very alone, very much a creature of solitude. I remember once at the books meeting at *Newsweek*, we were picking books and I decided I was going to write about Toni Cade Bambara's *The Sea Birds Are Still Alive*. This particularly snide editor was leafing through it and said, '*The Sea Birds Are Still Alive* — does anybody care?' Those kinds of possibly genuinely offhand remarks sent you screaming into a black colleague's office, or would just plunge the heart, and surround you with that kind of angry defensiveness as you did your work. So we really needed some handholding. There are so many forms of resistance and recalcitrance to feminist progress, to racial progress, et cetera. They're so flexible, they're so versatile!

TWR   Did those sorts of experiences at the beginning of your career inform your feminism? And do you think the workplace is progressing?
MJ   It's a little paradoxical, or maybe it's just a very predictable contradiction? Getting jobs was not difficult for me because women and blacks had been lobbying and threatening lawsuits a few years before I came. I basically got to *Newsweek* with very good writing samples, and having graduated first in my class from Columbia, but would I have been paid attention to as a job applicant if the women at *Newsweek* had not threatened to sue, and the settlement dictated that a certain group of women were promoted from inside? All quite qualified I might add. And another group of women were hired from outside. The *Times* had been put under exactly the same justified pressures, and I started freelancing for them in the eighties. I'd left *Newsweek* by then and I was teaching, but I was freelancing because I wanted to keep my voice, and my belief in more welcoming journalistic spaces. So I made a point of starting to freelance for the *Village Voice*'s literary supplement, *The Nation*, which I've always written for, and *Ms*. So the *Times* would come and court me at regular intervals when they were looking for black women in the arts, of whom very few were hired. I talked to them about coming on as an editor and as a critic, and several times I said no. And then in 1993 I said yes. For me, getting the job was less the problem because I benefited from social action. It was more these somewhat subtler cultural and psychological hostilities, as well as indifference. That was really what kept me constantly angry and analysing, asking, *what's going on here? What are the hierarchies?* It kept that part of me alive, as did constant conversation, not only with women in writing. In my generation, women were going into law firms for the first time; they were going into business; they were going into NGOs. Men, including some minorities, if they'd gotten enough class privilege, got certain kinds of training in how to deal with power in certain kinds of institutions, and I don't know any woman of any background of my generation who had that kind of training. Most of us, at least my friends, we wanted to keep our principles, so that training, learning how to negotiate it, how to fight it, but also how to fight — was incredibly worthwhile. I didn't want to just fight to review a cool white book. I wanted to fight for my right to review minority books, women's books, and any white book that I wanted to as well.

TWR   I love this quote from *Negroland*: 'We were to be ladies, responsible Negro women, and indomitable Black Women. We were not to be depressed or unduly high-strung... I craved the right to turn my face to the wall, to create a death commensurate with bourgeois achievement, political awareness, and aesthetically compelling feminine despair.' This section has deservedly been discussed a lot. I really like the idea of suicide as an act of rebellion against your upbringing and how society's trained you to exist as a woman. It made me think that, today, we're hyper-focused on certain issues within blackness, and those issues don't often include suicide and mental health. There might be critics who would say, who cares about suicide when things like police brutality exist? Especially today, when so much of the discussion about discrimination focuses on incarceration and this very brutal sort of violence and death that is completely out of our control as black people (and also focuses almost entirely on male victims.) For black people, what is the importance of having a space for our internal struggles and our fragility?

MJ   Maybe I'll go backwards and say, what is the suicide rate among incarcerated black men? Incarceration is a kind of emotional brutality and torture. If we look at centuries of white supremacy, and the toll of police brutality, the economy, structures and hierarchies of every form of social and legal injustice, how could we not also be looking at emotional abuse and brutality and those structural hierarchies that threaten and damage our collective psyches? Part of oppression, part of racism is, to me, a variety of attacks. Of course, they shift according to your position, what class protections you may have, what gender protections you may have, even what familial support you may have. But psychological abuse is a massive part of the system. I've found, especially among young people, a real interest in this airing of minority community mental health issues, and the state of neglect of treatments for it. The truth of black people's depression is that it is manifold and multiple and it takes every form at every strata of society. Now, I'm much better off than your typical prison inmate, male or female, but we'd be fools not to carefully analyse the ways in which even the most privileged among us have been socially, intellectually and emotionally attacked and damaged. That's our burden. We're also bringing that material to everything that we do, and our work gets read and attended to. And so it matters.

TWR   *Negroland* immediately struck me as a book that's not supposed to be written, because it airs some of our community's dirty laundry.

MJ   Which is why I had to put that on practically the first page, because I realised that if I didn't say I was basically brought up not to write this book right away, I might not ever get it made. Mental health is one of those issues that's considered dirty laundry. You will be punished by certain people, and importantly, you will have proven that racism has won, so you will be one of its victims, and that will also again damage our collective project of a kind of invincibility.

TWR   Yes, exactly. And the narrative of suicide, especially as you put it, directly contradicts that idea.

MJ   Hopefully, the book can also play some role in helping us look more realistically at the different kinds of damage that are done. Of course we all want a black narrative of progress, but maybe progress does not have to include stoic, warrior-like, invincible triumphs? Because it doesn't. If we look at our history, it doesn't. What are we going to make of that?

TWR   Much like your discussion of mental health, I found your discussion of class to be taboo-breaking and unexpected. Writing about privilege among African-Americans is something that is not really done anymore, and when you admit to your privilege, there are consequences that come to bear upon you. Privilege is almost seen as a disqualifier from an authentic black experience. Why is it important that we write about privilege among black people?

MJ   I would say it has something in common with why it's important to write about whiteness when it seems invisible. Invisibility is the mark of total accepted privilege — when it doesn't have to be talked about, when it's agreed upon that we don't need to discuss it because the status quo preserves it. One of the tactics of socially privileged people, contrary to the ones who showboat and build huge mansions, has been to close down the conversation of exactly what they have whenever they want to. They say, well, you know, we're just comfortable. We also see something different in the age of Trump, but it is usually the trope of so-called well-behaved WASP families. You would say, I don't really think there's such a thing as an upper class anymore, do you? That was the only reason they were being interviewed! I think among the 'best' black families, there is a certain pride, a kind of self-congratulation that magazines like *Ebony* used to stand for. Nevertheless, there is also a way in which black privileged people manage by virtue of genuine language — by participating in the Civil Rights movement, and by taking part in advancing black people on various fronts, actions that take attention away from the specifics of how privilege and the accumulation of wealth shape you. In a way, I'm taking the easy route by first sounding like a muck-raker, and I'm being righteous in saying we have to expose that privilege. But I also really feel that, again, one of the classic ways of dealing with an oppressed people is to reduce them to generalisations — to certain sentences, to ID tags, with declarations of what their main problems are. They get repeated over and over, and we have to keep making all of these distinctions and adjustments and identifications so that we can see all the ways in which we're rewarded, how we're deprived, how racial identity is a form of unity, where in fact it's a form of fractiousness and difference. Class plays a very, very big role in that. As a writer, I would also just say the more stories we have to tell, the better.

TWR   Can you talk about what criticism's importance is to you? Did you choose it as a form, or did it choose you? What is its power as a form?
MJ   I knew I wanted to write non-fiction, and I knew that I had a mind that wanted to analyse and place things. In that historical period of 1969-70, all of the things that interested me — a global non-white culture, feminism, and gay rights — everything was opening up. That was thrilling to me. I felt I could have a voice there. Critics analyse, yes, and we do 'criticise', but we dramatise too, we use our senses acutely. I wanted to make all this overlooked or newly emerging material come alive, and I also wanted to give it a place in the culture — with its canons and its long-sanctioned history — that it hadn't been given before. I wanted to create a collaborative, polyphonic culture.

TWR   Your memoir made me think about the identity of a critic. I sometimes contend with the stereotypes of a novelist — namely that we tend to be solitary, with fragile egos. I tend to think poets are more social and generally have more fun. Do you interact with these stereotypes of critics, and if so, do you think they apply to you?
MJ   There is this kind of play of omniscience, the performing of the omniscient narrator. But

a lot of us are also rattled by this sense that we're kind of at the bottom of the hierarchy you've just named. It used to make me crazy. I knew it was just a phrase or a trope, but it spoke to something when people would say, as they often still do, 'we're going to invite critics and writers'. I remember once saying to a writer friend of mine, who was writing journalism but also fiction, that critics are writers too! What interests me most now about criticism, and I'm sure we talked about this in class — criticism is vulnerability, it's ambivalence. It's being open to encountering a work with a combination of analytical and sensory material. How encountering a work or an idea doesn't have to close down to a series of conclusions, however fascinating, but it can open up to questions, strange little fractures and fissures. To me, that is what's most interesting about what a critic can do. Writing is always hard work, but as a critic you learn certain tricks, you learn certain ways of approaching the work, you learn what makes people impressed by and excited by your work and you just keep repeating that. One reason that that becomes so easy is because you're not exposing the parts of yourself that the work has really unsettled or rattled. How do you do that and remain interestingly coherent? How do you question yourself and offer a kind of implicit self-examination, which is, if not always, sometimes self-criticism?

TWR   Maybe part of the reason there's this bad, popular misconception of critics is because when people think of criticism, they think of little capsule book reviews where the critic hasn't read the book? But if they thought about your work, they would have a much better idea of what criticism is actually supposed to be.
MJ   I think that's always been true of criticism. It can be a serious, exploratory, sometimes experimental venture. It can be a form of literary or creative non-fiction. Some of it, in the sort of great marketplace, has always been and always will be just little capsule judgments that aren't necessarily stupid, but that are just meant to keep the consumers coming and going and the writer feeling on top of things. Listen, I've done pieces like that myself. I know the temptation of feeling in control, that I'm the mistress surveying and you're going to be punished.

TWR   As you said, *Negroland* is a memoir, but your critical voice is very much incorporated, on a sentence level, and there are some straight-forwardly critical passages. In writing the book, did you consciously shift from criticism into memoir-writing?

MJ   Initially, I was scared to death and desperate to get writing. So at first I would just do a scene: *I'm on a train, I'm 7 and my sister's 10...* Then I would do a confession about something else. I did a little portrait of one of my parents. I was always collect-ing historical materials, so I'd do something about a black neighbourhood. I was collecting these scenes, but when I tried to find a shape I couldn't quite do it. Now, that's partly because memoirs often have a very definite chronology, and though there is some chronology in mind, there's a lot of digression and veering. I had to come to realise that a narrative voice that's as identifiable as the lead character in a play or novel, and that you often find in a shapely memoir, was not going to work for me. I was taught to play a lot of different roles, and to manage a lot of personae. That had to be a part of my voice. That was my first really helpful realisation. Then I started enumerating all these personae: the good daughter, the good student in a white school, the kid who went to a white school and who wants to be very cool at a black party. And then I suddenly thought, wait a minute, I've been a critic since the 1970s. This is part of my sen-sibility. It is as much a part of my identity as all this other stuff and it has to be there. I also realised that every book needs sources of tension, and I already had some, but I thought, oh my god: I'm enact-ing it. Now I have to make it consciously work in terms of the shape and the prose. The tension between Margo the critic, Margo the actor, Margo the confessor, Margo the mediator, Margo the loyalist, Margo the good girl. And how does Margo the critic respond to all of those? When does she recede and when does she advance? I change tones quickly, without necessarily explaining that I'm going to change my tone now; instead I invite the reader to watch me offer a different performance.

TWR   I was quite struck by the continuity in writing style between *Negroland* and your other writing. It felt like the same voice — your natural voice — applied differently. I saw it even in your first book, *On Michael Jackson*.

MJ   *On Michael Jackson* was a transition for me from a critical voice that was mine, but that was still working within what I'll call the house styles of publications I'd worked for. It was also very aware of the audience. One reason I wanted to do the Michael Jackson book was to claim more of the critic's voice itself, free of these other external con-ditions. After Michael Jackson, people kept saying I should write about Beyoncé or Prince next, and I would think, I don't want to do that at all! I wanted to push further. I wanted to try something new. I wanted to dig, and that's when I began to think about a memoir. People would say, why don't you write about that mysterious world you came from? But I hadn't taken it seriously. It's the oldest story in the book for us writers: what I might not be able to do, but I'm determined to do.

Z. C.,
June 2018

ALLISON KATZ

'Painting is a conversation,' Allison Katz told *The White Review* in 2015. Attempting to keep pace is an exhilarating challenge. Within her work, Katz sets up puckish chains of association: a way of ensuring that meaning is always on the move. She generates content from often dissonant historical styles and sources, and frequently references her earlier work. Visual and linguistic plays abound, often making use of the markers of her identity, including her name, signature, and bodily features, which appear in various guises. By working against the torpor of nostalgia and convention, Katz sidesteps many of painting's dead ends – among them, the cult of hyper-individual expression that dominated much of modern painting, seduction by any single style, or the recent propensity to ape the flatness of the digital screen. Since 2009 Katz has created approximately 100 posters for solo and group exhibitions in which her work features. This issue contains a selection of Katz's posters to date, as well as a newly commissioned edition for the cover. The posters are considered artworks in their own right, and extend beyond the role of supplement or messenger. They may be sent out as announcements, printed in different sizes, displayed alongside paintings as individual works and as small and large editions, given away for free, printed after the exhibition has closed, or exist solely as jpegs. Multiple iterations are often produced for a single show, and dates, names, and locations are treated as elements to be abstracted. The presentation of her posters at Billedrommet, Norway in 2017 was the first instance of Katz's graphic practice being exhibited independently. Also on show was a collaged box, designed to store the archive, decorated to reflect previous themes while developing new ones. The posters are the result of an entirely digital process, using snapshots taken by Katz and created using graphic design software. They continue her interest in toying with the tenets of painting, and its display: extending the realm of the work beyond the cloistered space and finite duration of the exhibition, and complicating the hierarchies of medium, material and motivation.

PLATES

I   *Le Tit*, 2010
II   *The Parts (Menagerie [The Century])*, 2011
III   *fig-futures (Split)*, 2018
IV   *Perra Perdida (Found in Quebec)*, 2013
V   *Shelf Painting Poster 3*, 2016
VI   *Daymark (Opening)*, 2012
VII   *AKgraph*, 2013
VIII   *Last seen entering the Biltmore*, 2014
IX   *Antenna Space at Paris Internationale (Caveman)*, 2017
X   *fig-2 week 47/50*, 2015
XI   *Rumours, Echoes (Alfama)*, 2014
XII   *The Song Cave Press Edition No. 6*, 2014
XIII   *Diary w/o Dates (Mum as Nippy)*, 2018
XIV   *Diary w/o Dates (Adult Services)*, 2018
XV   *We boil at different degrees*, 2016

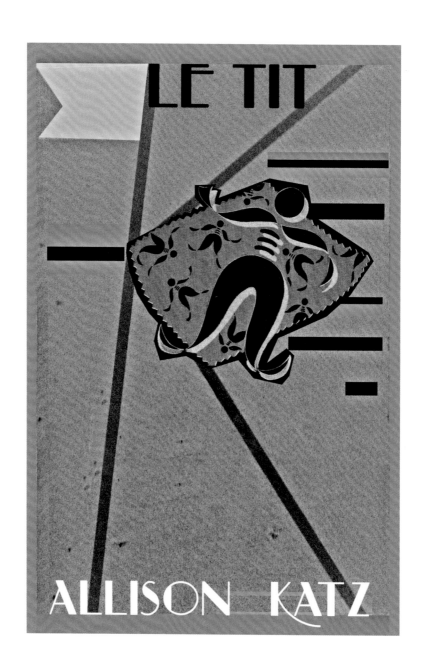

LE TIT

ALLISON KATZ

THE PARTS JOHAN BERGGREN GALLERY MALMÖ SE
JUNE 4 - JULY 16 2011

ALLISON KATZ

FIG.-FUTURES

BLACKPOOL

ALK ALLATSON

1/5 · 5/5 · 2013

GRUNDY ART GALLERY

CHIENNE PERDUE

RÉCOMPENSE 100$

LULU
5526953341

AK & FV

ALL
AR8UND

AMATEUR

Bergen Kunsthall NO 26.05.16 - 14.08.16
Le Consortium Dijon FR 18.11.16 - 19.02.17

ALLISON KATZ

DAYMARK

last seen entering the Biltmore

South London Gallery

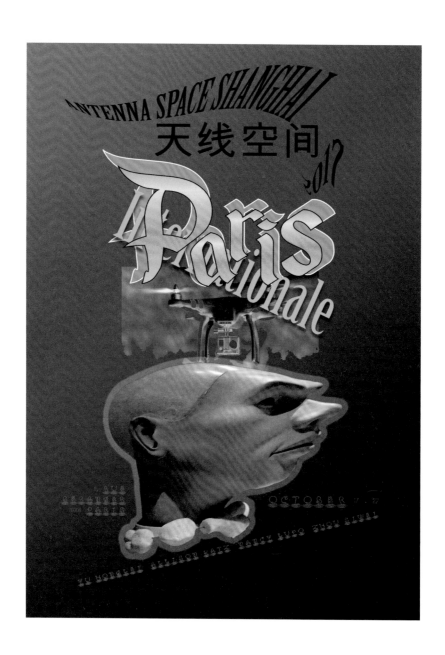

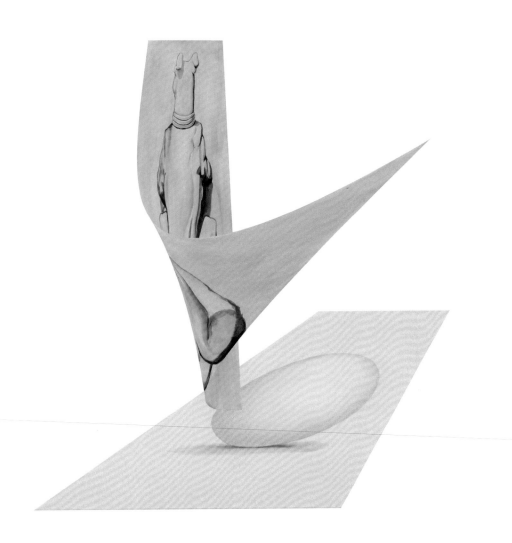

BOATOS

RUA JOÃO MOURA 187
SÃO PAULO
RUMOURS
ECHOES
ALLISON 4/9-4/10
KATZ 2014

the song cave

EDITION NO 6

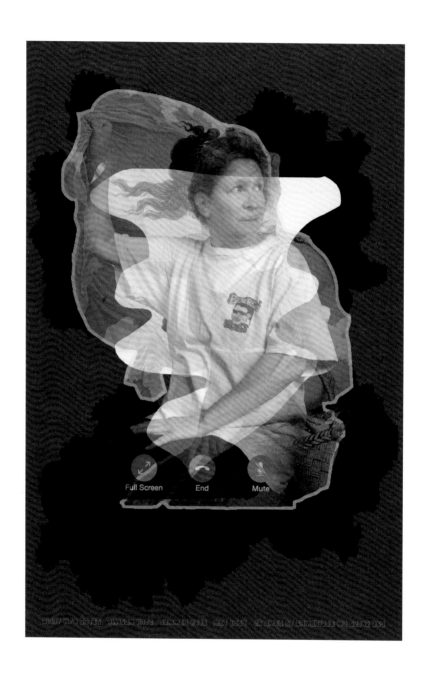

Full Screen   End   Mute

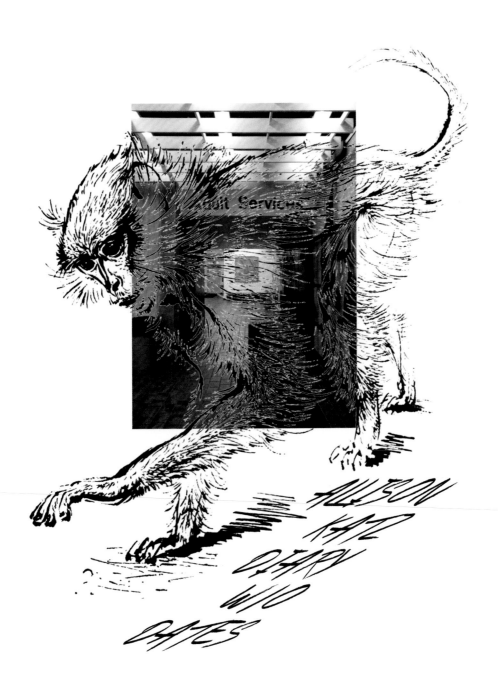

THE GREAT AWAKE
JULIA ARMFIELD

FICTION

When I was 27, my Sleep stepped out of me like a passenger from a train carriage, looked around my room for several seconds, then sat down in the chair beside my bed. This was before they became so familiar, the shadow-forms of Sleep in halls and kitchens, before the mass displacement left so many people wakeful at uncertain hours of the night. In those days, it was still surprising to sit up and see the silver lean of Sleep, its casual elbows. People rang one another, apologising for the lateness, asking friends if they too were playing host to uninvited guests.

Sleep was always tall and slender but beyond that there were few common traits. Experiences varied – a girl I knew complained that her Sleep sat ceaselessly atop her chest of drawers, swinging its heels and humming, while another confided that her Sleep trailed its fingers down her calves, demanding cones of mint ice cream. Couples and cohabiters were the worst off – the Sleeps seemed more prone to behaving badly in numbers, as though they were egging one another on. A rumour persisted in my building that the husband and wife in the penthouse had locked their Sleeps in separate bathrooms to prevent them wrestling violently on the carpet. A man I knew vaguely from the office told me in passing that his and his boyfriend's Sleeps kicked at one another incessantly and flicked pieces of rolled-up paper at the neighbour's Bengal cat. My Sleep had no one to fight with and so mostly preoccupied itself with rooting through my personal belongings, pulling out old photographs and allen keys and defunct mobile phones, then placing them like treasures at the foot of my bed.

Early on, we didn't know what it was exactly. A lot of people assumed they were seeing ghosts. One night in mid-July, a woman in my building woke the seventh floor with her shrieking. 2 a.m., dark throat of summer. A bleary stagger of us collected in the corridor and were beckoned into her flat in our sleeping shorts and dressing gowns. We walked from room to room, near-strangers despite our daily proximity, taking furtive note of her decor and her sloppy housekeeping, the cereal bowls on the coffee table, the dirty novel on the bed. We found it in the bedroom, moon-drenched through open curtains. Her Sleep was lanky, crouched beside the bookshelf. It must have been the first time any of us had seen one – its wraithish fingers and ungentle mouth. I remember that the girl beside me grabbed my hand when she saw it. She was a girl I knew by sight but had never spoken to – still sticky with sleep around the eyelids and wearing the type of mouthguard prescribed by dentists for bruxism. I squeezed her hand in return and tried to make sense of what I was looking at. The Sleep crossed its palms across its neck as though protecting the feeblest part of itself from harm.

The newspapers labelled it *The Great Awake*, printed graphs and pie charts and columns by confused academics. News pundits speculated broadly, blaming it on phones and social media, 24-hour culture, anxiety disorders in the under-18s. Radio hosts blamed it on television. Talking heads on television blamed it on everybody else. Ultimately, there was found to be little concrete evidence behind any one cause – it wasn't more likely to happen if you ate meat or drank coffee or had extra-marital sex. It wasn't a virus or a medical syndrome, it had nothing to do with the drinking water or women being on the pill. It happened in cities, that much we knew, though beyond that there was no obvious pattern. It could happen to one house on a city street and not another. It could affect everyone in an apartment building except for you. It was described more commonly as a phenomenon than as a disaster; one medical journal referred to it as an amputation of sorts, the removal of the sleep-state from the body. People wrote in to magazines to describe their symptoms: the sudden persistent wakefulness, the mutation of sleep from a comforting habit to a creature that crouched by the door.

Fairly early on, a live morning show with a viewership of some four million was yanked unceremoniously off air because the host had been attempting to present a segment on seasonal salads with his Sleep in shot behind him. The figure was only a little taller than average and mimed laconically along to the host's actions, shadowing him as he reached for tomatoes while lecturing viewers on proper knife technique. The Sleep mimicked a paring knife, chopping smoothly at the air. It was a Tuesday, people ironing shirts before work. I remember the squeal and stutter before the screen cut to a placard reading *Technical Difficulties - Please Stand By*. I remember the host's eyes, the wakeful crescents beneath the lids. In time, of course, this kneejerk plug-pulling became impractical. By the following month, half the media personalities in the schedule were turning up to work with wan faces and their Sleeps in tow. A new series of a property show started with one of the two hosts introducing her Sleep quite candidly, her co-host standing off to the side alone. Television became a gradual sea of doubles, of familiar faces and their silent, unaccustomed companions. It became so swiftly ordinary — not a thing to be longed for, but nothing whatsoever to be done. Like the chicken pox, ungrimly inevitable. People slept until their Sleeps stepped out of them, then they went on living awake. Shortly after our first encounter on the seventh floor, people in my building stopped sleeping at a rate of about one a night. Mine appeared early, an awkward guest to whom I first thought to offer tea or the newspaper, though I quickly discovered that Sleep was not a companion who wanted much entertaining; it preferred to roam the flat in silence, straightening picture frames where they had fallen askew. I continued to talk to it despite little indication that what I said was appreciated, occasionally replying to myself in a different voice to keep the conversation going. I told my Sleep it reminded me of Peter Pan's shadow, and wondered aloud whether I ought to try to attach it to me with a bar of carbolic soap. My Sleep only shook its shoulders and pulled the clock from the kitchen wall to adjust it with a gentle nudge to the minute hand. 'Yes, maybe you should,' I said in a different voice and nodded to show that I had heard. Later on, it transpired that no one's Sleeps would speak to them. A strange enough curse, to be wide awake with a companion who pretended you weren't there.

My brother called, quoting our mother — *only think about what moving to the city will do to your health.* His Sleep had appeared only two hours previously and was pacing round the kitchen, rattling chairs and humming the theme to a radio soap for which my brother had once unsuccessfully auditioned.

'Janey, does yours look anything like grandad?'

I squinted sideways at my Sleep, its steam-coloured skin.

'I don't think so. If anything, it looks like Aunt Lucy, but that's because the only time I saw her was at the open casket.'

My brother chuckled; a muffled sound, hand hovered over the mouthpiece. It was three o'clock in the morning, heavy-lidded sky.

'Pretty spooky,' he said. 'Plus kind of a bore. There's nothing on TV this time of night.'

When we were younger, our mother told us warning stories about the pro-liferation of ghosts in big cities; ghosts in office chairs and office bathrooms, hot and cold running ghosts on tap. Cupping an ear to the evening stillness of our rural home, she would describe to us towns that seethed with spectres, mime the permanent unsettlement of a city night. These stories, intended as a deterrent to leaving, quickly became the basis of our preferred childhood games. Collecting cardboard boxes and empty tupperware containers, we would fashion knee-high cities in the basement and chase phantoms around their miniature alley-ways, stacking books into the shapes of high-rise apartments and imagining them jittery with ghosts. When the two of us grew up and moved away – to our long thin city of narrow stairs and queasy chimney stacks – our mother cried and demanded we reconsider, insisting that cities could not be lived in but only haunted, that we would simply become two more ghosts in a place where ghosts already abound.

An interview ran in a Sunday broadsheet: a young woman studying history at university, who described the experience of falling in love with her Sleep:

He's a great listener, a great talker. (I call him 'He' – I don't know if that's politically correct or possible, but that's what he feels like to me.) People say their Sleeps don't talk but I wonder whether that's just because they're expecting speech in the traditional sense. My Sleep doesn't make any noise but that doesn't mean he doesn't talk to me. There are gestures - he moves to the corner of the mattress to give me more space, he alphabetises my books. Sometimes he touches my forehead. Talk can be all kinds of things.

I read this article aloud to my Sleep, asked it whether it was trying to talk to me and I was just too preoccupied by its silence to hear, though of course I received no response.

'I think mine might just be a bit of an arsehole,' my brother said. He was drowsy the way we were all becoming, plum smudges in the hollows of his eyes. 'It hides my scripts and scribbles all over my calendar. I've missed three auditions because it's scratched out the dates. It's like living with a shitty poltergeist.'

We were sitting on the front steps of my building, drinking hot choco-late from polystyrene cups. It was 4 a.m. on a Tuesday; thin light, city moving like an agitated creature. We were all still growing used to the night-time, the blue-veined hours of morning that lay only lightly, the white spiders and noctule bats. Without sleeping, it was harder to parcel up your days, to maintain a sense of urgency. The extra hours granted a kind of fearless laziness, a permission to dawdle through the day with the confidence that there would be more time, later, whenever you liked.

'I don't think mine likes me very much,' I said to my brother, finishing my hot chocolate and reaching for the dregs of his. 'It always seems so distracted.'

My brother shrugged, squinting down towards the bottom of the steps where our Sleeps were jostling elbows and kicking at each other's feet.

The girl with the mouthguard knocked on my door one midnight in mid-September and asked me to come and confirm something for her. She was wearing a nightdress – I had torn mine up for dishcloths, having little other use for it – though she had taken the mouthguard out and was holding it gingerly in one hand when I opened the door. Without it, her voice was a curiously clean thing, freshly scrubbed, as though all of her teeth were brand new. Her flat across the corridor was the direct reversal of mine; the kitchen sink and cupboards facing in the opposite direction, the books strewn about in seeming parallel to the ones that littered my bed. It turned out that what she had imagined, on waking, to be the shape of her Sleep in the corner of her bedroom was in fact only the shadow of her dressing gown thrown over a chair. And what she had assumed to be the sound of her Sleep shifting about beside the bookcase was only the rattle of mice in the walls. She was disappointed, bleary from waking. Everyone in her family already had one, she told me. She went to sleep every night and felt like she was missing out on something, this all-night party she was too exhausted to attend.

'What's stupid is I've always been a very troubled sleeper,' she said, gesturing to her mouthguard. 'You'd think I would have been one of the first.'

Her name was Leonie and when she talked she beat her hands together with a sound like popping corn. She wore the mouthguard to correct excessive tooth-grinding owing to an abnormal bite – an affliction she'd lived with since her late teens when she had lost her back teeth crashing her bicycle into a stationary car. This she told me lightly before blinking and apologising for the overshare, though I only shook my head. I had found that people seemed to speak more freely in the night-time – a strange release of inhibitions that came with talking in the dark. I left a message for our building's maintenance department about the mice in her wall and sat with her until she fell asleep the wrong way up on top of her bedclothes. She was pretty, a fact I noticed in a guilty, thieving way. She had fine buttery hair and a gentle cleft in her chin. My Sleep, which had followed me across the corridor and into the flat, oversaw all of this with no particular interest, wandering about and pulling lampshades off their stands.

You don't notice the way a city breathes until it changes its sleeping habits. Looking downwards, you could see it – the restlessness of asphalt. I liked to watch from my window for the heave of sundown, the roll and shrug of something searching for a comfortable way to lie. My brother rang, on his way to an audition which had been rescheduled for two in the morning – an early example of what would become the fairly common practice of 'repurposing the night'.

'We're all awake anyway, so why not use the time,' he said, voice blurry from his warm-up exercises. I listened to him run through his audition piece, covering my mouth to stifle a yawn. After he hung up, I leant far out of my window and watched a gang of small girls from the building playing football in the street. Their Sleeps ran alongside them, sticking out unsporting legs and yanking at their ponytails. I stayed there for a long time with the night heavy on my eyelids, the whole world hushed and hot beyond my windowsill.

Leonie took to knocking for me at midnight; little Bastille knocks which I answered in the leisurely way I now did everything, sometimes setting a pot of coffee to steep before I came to the door. Perhaps in a bid to lure her Sleep out into the open, she had put away her old nightclothes and usually came over in soft blue jeans and work shirts. She was a writer, she told me, she wrote an agony column for a newspaper I occasionally read. She had an overcaffeinated rattle about her, a slight urgency to her widened eyes that begged me not to ask if she was feeling tired. Occasionally, I would catch her staring enviously at my Sleep, unconsciously mimicking its gestures. She was tired of tiredness, she told me. She was tired of feeling left out.

We quickly developed a sort of routine, the way we knew many people in our building had begun to arrange their night-times. A woman who lived on the ground floor had started walking her Sleep around the park every night in what we saw as a vain attempt to tire it out. A cellist who lived in the flat directly above me had put together a nightly chamber group along with a viola player who lived on the second floor and the couple from the penthouse, both of whom were apparently amateur violinists. Leonie and I met at midnight, usually in my flat. We did nothing very momentous together – we ate mustard on toast and listened to late night radio, played solitaire, read our horoscopes and the palms of one another's hands. Sometimes, she brought fragments of her work over and sat on the floor with her back against the sofa, reading me letters the paper had sent her to answer, determinedly suppressing her yawns.

'Listen to this one,' was her usual refrain, affecting the voices of her letter-writers. A teenage girl who was too shy to masturbate with her Sleep watching. A university student whose Sleep stood in front of the door in the mornings and made it impossible to go to class. A man who complained that his wife had a Sleep and he didn't – a situation which he felt undermined his standing in the relationship. This last Leonie read aloud with her tongue pressed downwards, in a voice which dripped contempt but left her face impassive. *She doesn't say she has a Sleep because she works harder and needs the extra hours awake, but I feel the judgement is implicit.*

'I wonder if it's unethical,' she said to me once. 'For me to be answering these letters when I don't have a Sleep myself.'

'No more than it is to offer a solution to any problem that isn't yours,' I replied, though she acted as if she hadn't heard me.

No matter how hard she tried, she could never stave off tiredness entirely. Our nights together often ended with her wilting on my sofa, jerking awake at 6 a.m. to insist that she had not been sleeping. I tended not to pass comment on this, any more than I chose to question her nightly invasions. I found I liked her company more than that of my Sleep, and vaguely resented the longing looks I would catch her stealing of the oblivious figure in the corner of the room. Sometimes when she left to get ready for work, she would kiss me on the cheek or the corner of my mouth, and I would go to get changed with damp lines along the centres of my palms.

The nights were strange-hued, liver-coloured things. A late September heat pressed downwards – damp pad of fingers at the base of a neck – and I spent my small hours drifting around the flat in shorts and T-shirts, listening to Leonie reading letters by people desperate to have sex with their Sleeps, or with each other's. When she was finished choosing which letters she would reply to during the day, we would talk or read together. She described things in odd ways – *the night gnawing on the windowsill, the pepper taste of her overchewed lip* – and I talked to her about things that amused me. I told her that Evelyn Waugh's first wife had also been named Evelyn and that the guy who voiced the Bugs Bunny cartoon had been allergic to carrots. She nodded along to what I said in a way that made me less inclined to bombard my Sleep with conversation in the hours she wasn't there. I had bad teeth and envied her sparse, white mouthful, like little cowrie shells that always seemed a trifle slick. She told me that they were only that small because she had ground them down so much. One reason she was so desperate for a Sleep of her own was that permanent wakefulness would save her from chewing the teeth right out of her mouth. Her voice, I came to realise, was a little like the voice I affected when miming my Sleep's replies to my questions, and I liked it very much. Most nights, when she could no longer control the weary bobbing of her head and fell asleep on my shoulder, I would let her stay there and get away with her sheepish claim, when she awoke, that she had only been resting her eyes.

My brother called to tell me he'd been cast in a play and I met him for drinks to celebrate. We drank red wine which stained our lips the same colour as the spaces beneath our eyes and he shouted his elation to the overcrowded bar. Public places were starting to smell of sleep, of unwashed linens. My brother upset his mostly empty glass in a re-enactment of his audition. His Sleep imitated the gesture, gesticulating none too kindly behind his back until he turned around and caught it.

'And you've been no help at all,' he told it, slurring gently, before turning back to continue his speech with an overdone archness. '*Macbeth doth murder sleep.* Eh?'

Later, I came home to find Leonie waiting for me with an armload of letters and a plate of coconut biscuits. She said she was itching to tell me a story about a girl she knew who worked for the same newspaper and had attended a series of seminars led by a woman who professed to know the secret to getting rid of a Sleep. Too much tea was the cause of it, the woman had warned, and an overreliance on artificial stimulus. Blue lights. Cut them out. Detox from dairy. The woman had sat in the centre of a circle of chairs, her Sleeplessness on full display as her students' Sleeps wandered around the room. 'Like a game of duck duck goose,' the girl from the newspaper had said. At the end of the fourth seminar, it had transpired that the woman running things had locked her Sleep in a broom cupboard to support the illusion that she had rid herself of it with only water and vegan cheese. Several members of the group had heard it beating on the walls during a cigarette break and had broken the lock on the door trying to get it out.

'People shouldn't be allowed them if they can't treat them properly,' Leonie said after she had finished telling the story, offering me a coconut biscuit. She looked unconvinced when I told her it was best not to think of them like dogs.

I read an article by a woman mourning the loss of her unconsciousness. The writer talked about her sleep before it became a capital: the relief of absence, the particular texture of the tongue and weight of the head after a night of sleeping well. *Sleeping gave me time off from myself - a delicious sort of respite. Without it I grow overfamiliar, sticky with self-contempt.* The article was published in Leonie's paper and as she read it I watched for her envy, the white of her knuckles as she clutched at the corners of the newspaper. The writer described her Sleep as smelling like smoke and honey, recounted its movements around her house: *The waft, the restless up-and-down. It throws tennis balls at the walls the way they do in prison break movies, kicks at the legs of my chairs.* Leonie asked me what my Sleep smelled like and I told her: orange peel and photo water. Odd, talismanic scents - my mother loading me down with tangerines for my journey to the city, sending me photographs of our old house in the post. A little later, having left the room to put on the kettle, I came back to find Leonie standing by my Sleep as it rooted through the boxes I kept under the bookcase. Not noticing me, she moved in as close as she could, tilted her head towards my Sleep and breathed in. I watched this happen for several seconds, watched the way my Sleep quirked its head in irritation but failed to pull away. Still breathing in, she rested her forehead against its neck for a fraction of a second and I imagined the sensation, cold glass wet with condensation against her skin.

The morning trains were overloaded with bodies both solid and spectral. I became used to standing whilst my Sleep muscled its way to a seat, grew accustomed to the rows of Sleeps with their legs crossed, the people clustered round the doors, grey-faced and leaning heavily. I spent lunchtimes wandering the city, watching people shuffle from coffee shops to street bodegas - the greasy slink of cooked meat, egg sandwiches. I sat on steps and municipal benches, eating the orange cake my mother sent from home in tin foil packages, talking to my brother on the phone.

Leonie read me a letter, leaning up against my fridge one night with her reading glasses on. She had taken to wearing them more often in recent weeks, whether or not she happened to be reading. It prevented her eyes getting tired so quickly, she said, in a rare moment of admission that tiredness was something she felt. It was difficult for her, this unnatural wakefulness. Occasionally she would look up from her writing desk during the day and swear she saw the city moving past the window, as though either it or she were running very fast in one direction.

'Our relationship is struggling,' read the letter, 'because of my husband's Sleep. Sometimes his expression when I wake in the night scares me. He says some nights he leans over me and tries to will my Sleep out of me so that we can both be awake together. I sometimes feel I must be the only person in the city left asleep, though I still feel tired all the time, which in itself he considers a kind of betrayal.'

Leonie came to sit beside me and laid her head down on my shoulder for a long time. It was hard, she said, to be sympathetic to all the people who wrote to her complaining of problems with their Sleeps, whilst at the same time feeling so bitterly conscious that there were still people like her left sleeping through the nights in this restless city. It made her worry that there was no countdown to zero, that some people might simply be destined to never have a Sleep at all. I told her that I didn't know what she thought she was hoping for, that I considered my Sleep an unfriendly interloper at best. I told her that sometimes I lay down on my bed and imagined unconsciousness, lay on one arm and then another until they lost all feeling and I could at least enjoy the sensation of sleep in some small part of my body. I told her that the only thing I really liked about my new situation was her company – that and the occasional thought of the city holding me up despite how tired I felt, like hands beneath my arms and around my middle, keeping me off the floor. Of course, by the time I said any of this she was already asleep on my shoulder, snoring gently into my neck. Above us, the string quartet played a Dvořák nocturne, a slow movement in B.

My mother called to check I was eating properly and to say she'd warned me something like this would happen. She didn't have a Sleep, of course. Very few people outside the city limits did. My mother's voice on the phone was well-rested, excessively virtuous. She told me she knew a man who lived not a stone's throw away from her who had gone into the city one day on business and returned with a Sleep which didn't belong to him. I asked her what had happened to the person whose Sleep had been stolen and my mother told me not to ask stupid questions. 'What do I know about the horrible things? I should imagine they're glad to be shot of it.' She asked after my brother, complaining that he never answered her calls. She asked me what I was doing with myself, whether I was seeing anyone, and I thought of telling her about Leonie, but my Sleep chose that moment to take the receiver away from me and hang up, apparently irritated by all the noise.

I asked Leonie if she wanted to come with me to see my brother's play and she nodded, resting her hand on my thigh for a moment and digging in her nails the way a cat might. She was sleepy around the eyes and the downcurve of her mouth and when she shifted towards me she smelled of hard city water. We were eating oranges on the sofa and she kept offering me pieces, though I had my own aproned out in my lap. The performance had been scheduled for two in the morning to capitalise on the night-time crowds. Leonie gamely brought along a flask of coffee and we sat in the dark together in the little raked space above a pub, sharing a box of chocolate-covered raisins and nudging each other every time my brother came on. On the stage, the actor's Sleeps performed what looked like their own play in the spaces behind them. Without dialogue, their storyline was hard to follow but it kept drawing my eye – the translucent figures shifting about around the actors, miming along to words I couldn't hear. It was nearly five by the time we got home and Leonie had finished her flask of coffee, eyes melting down her face. I asked her if she wanted to come in but she told me she needed her mouthguard, looking away in embarrassment and flashing her fingers by way of farewell. Less than an hour later, she knocked on my door again, complaining of nightmares. It was relentless, she told me, like everyone else's unused dreams now came to bother her, bringing nightmares of fast-climbing vines and empty trains and soil fertile with teeth. I let her sleep on my sofa with her head pillowed in my lap until seven, when I had to start dressing for work. Moving between rooms with my toothbrush in one hand, I glimpsed her sitting up on the sofa, peeling another orange and offering slices to my Sleep.

One night, Leonie asked me to proofread something she was writing. I had a better eye for detail, she said, I was used to reading in the dark. The piece wasn't for her advice column but one she had been asked to write for a magazine – an article on living without a Sleep, she told me with a grimace. She'd write it anonymously, she said. It wasn't something she wanted to own. Towards the end of the piece, she described it as like the sensation of looking for your shadow on the ground in front of you only to realise it was nowhere to be found; of looking around you and finding the sun just where it was supposed to be, of seeing the shadows stretching away from the feet of everyone but you.

'It's a good piece,' I said, when I'd read it. 'But you're writing like you're making it up. Like it's fiction and you're trying to imagine how someone like you must feel.'

'Wishful thinking,' she replied, as my Sleep entered the room from the kitchen, rattling its fingertips across the top of the radiator.

She shrugged a shoulder and raised her head to look at me, leaning forwards after a moment to kiss me on the side of my mouth, nodding her thanks. I dipped my chin, tilting slightly to catch her properly on the mouth and she kissed me gently for a moment before pulling away. She smiled at me vaguely, shrugged her other shoulder, and I realised she tasted like oranges.

My brother called to tell me to turn on Channel 4. He was watching a news piece on people who were doing drastic things to rid themselves of Sleep. They interviewed a woman who had been arrested for luring her Sleep to the top of her apartment building and pushing it off. The way it fell, she said, you would have thought it didn't know about gravity. The legs continuing to walk through nothing, the windmill before the sudden dragging drop. This woman was the only one who had agreed to be interviewed without insisting her face be pixelated. She had been released from police custody, there being no workable law in place to condemn her, but was largely housebound due to the protesters surrounding her property and forcing hate mail through the letterbox.

'When I retell it,' she said, *'I have to remind myself that what I did wasn't unnatural. No more than taking a pill to fall asleep is unnatural.'*

The noise from her front lawn could be heard inside the house, the chants picked up on the reporter's microphone. Even so, she seemed singularly unbothered. As the interview drew to a close, she tilted her head towards the window and the sunlight hit her in a way which illuminated the spaces beneath her eyes, fresh as new-poured paint, gloriously well-rested.

'Makes you think, doesn't it?' my brother said, once the news had moved on to another story. *'Not a nice thought, but makes you think.'*

'I didn't know you could kill them,' I replied. No one had known until now, it seemed, because no one had really tried. 'It doesn't seem right though, does it?'

Leonie's piece was published anonymously and she brought the magazine around at midnight. The story was sandwiched between several others; the man who had stolen another man's Sleep, the woman who had packed her Sleep into the back of a car, driven it out to the country and left it there. Leonie's piece, I thought, sat oddly amongst these stories of frayed nerves and hard exhaustion. In the midst of all these haunted people, she sat alone, without a ghost yet longing for one, her writing like a clasp of fingers around empty air. I reread the piece while she made me tea, the gentle clatter of her in the other room a pleasant thing, just as the restlessness of the night had become a comforting familiarity. City noise, the wriggle of wakeful shoulders, Leonie breaking a cup and cursing to herself next door.

When she came back, she was white, red-lipped from biting at herself. My Sleep came after her, holding the pieces of the mug she had broken, which it ferried to the coffee table and placed there before moving to the corner of the room. Leonie passed me a cup of tea and came to sit beside me, eyeing the magazine in my hands.

'I hate it,' she said, 'I wish I hadn't written it.' Her voice curled up around its edges the way paper does when you set it alight at the sides. I looked at her dumbly for a moment, sipped my tea on a reflex and immediately burned my tongue.

In the corner, my Sleep twitched its head to the side. An odd motion, as though trying to get water out of its ears. I looked at Leonie and thought about the heaviness at her shoulders, picturing the sensation of sleeping, the fall and sudden absence of thought. After we'd finished our tea, I asked her to lie down on the sofa with me. She looked at me strangely but didn't object. We positioned ourselves as comfortably as possible, Leonie slipping up into the crook of my arms. I pictured sleep – the old stillness and the blacks of my own closed eyes. In the corner, my Sleep shifted itself, turning its head into its own shoulder, then the crook of its elbow, as if to inhale a smell.

'I should have my mouthguard,' Leonie murmured vaguely, though I only shushed her, saying after a moment that I'd wake her if she started spitting teeth.

I held her for a long time and, after the night had passed, woke up to find that I had slept. The corner of my room was empty, as was the space before me on the sofa. Leonie had gone, leaving behind the magazine but taking with her my Sleep. The magazine lay the way we had left it, folded over to a piece by a woman whose Sleep seemed desperate to get away from her. Leonie had read it aloud to me, the low blur of her voice broken up by gentle exhalations: '*The feeling is one of rejection, of course, but more than that, a desperate wrongness, a subversion of whatever we now claim counts as the natural state. I lock it up in the bathroom and it claws at the doorframe. I leave it alone for two seconds and it makes for the window ledge. Often it occurs to me that I ought just to let it go, but the paralysing question, of course, is what will happen to me then? If my Sleep leaves, will I sleep? Or will I simply be left awake and drifting, abandoned by the strange companion who allows this to make sense?*'

Alone on the sofa, I chose not to sit up, remaining instead where I was for a long time and registering the renewed lightness of my body, the gentle swimming ease of an object which has been relieved at last of its heaviest component. I was more than usually aware of my arms, my legs, the freedom with which I felt suddenly sure I could lift them. A little later, I would rise and go about my business, noting when I did so the old sensation of restoration, a certain softness in places where I had previously felt bound by gravity. I would revel in this feeling for a moment, the lifting from the tops of my shoulders and from my back, before catching sight of the place on the coffee table where Leonie had left her mug and feeling something rather different – still a lifting, but something less welcome and more like the removal of a well-liked hand from my arm. I would feel this and look swiftly over to the empty corner, but for now I remained where I was. It was morning, the air refreshed and gentle as if from dreamless sleep.

REBECCA GOSS

POETRY

NOMENCLATURE
For Dr Rebecca Goss, Professor in Organic/
Biomolecular Chemistry, University of St Andrews

How long did we look at our mothers
from the safe ledge of their hips,
hear the word *Rebecca* spoken, whispered,
(all that soothing, pointing)
until eventually its hard, end-vowel
caused the turn of our heads?
Loved for its length, something to offset
our surname's syllabic lack, it suited us.
We were firstborns. We were Rebeccas.
We grew our hair long and straight.
With eager grips on Berol, this shared appellation
practised on pages of feint-rule; school
shaping us into very different women.
In Chemistry, your teacher made sugar syrup
for his bees, you witnessed the substances
of which matter is composed. Science
declared itself to you. Me, I was a smoker,
occasional truant, but really a good girl,
unable to resist when a teacher placed Faulkner
in my hand. I'm ahead of you by two years,
reached certain freedoms and discoveries earlier.
University. Motherhood. I got to write
our name inside the covers of slim books.
You weren't far behind me, on dance floors
that stirred you until late, with lovers,
knowledge forming its ziggurat in you.
What do I really know of this?
I know your daughter raised her head
when she was born, locked eyes with you in a stare
as you held her shining, intended body.
I know because you wrote it down,
out of all the things you could have told me
and knowing it has made me realise
what we both have,
finds me turning back to reach for you.

YOUR PALM IS A FLAG
After Alison Watt 'Flexion' (2003)

Your palm is a flag
above heads of others
so I can locate the square of this earth
where you stand
and I nod, raise my arm.
We converse by stretch of limb.
As I nudge past shoulders
towards you, a recent morning
comes clear in my mind, when
I broke open the curtains
reachable with an outstretched
hand from our bed, the damp transfer
of condensation revealed, obscuring
our view of the walnut tree.
One night's humidity
declaring itself.
Droplets on cold glass — proof
of temperature, pressure, touch
(all things we have
known each other by)
causing the angles
of our sleepy bodies to contract,
a reluctance
to be upright, or
tall as you are now
in this crowd, beckoning.

FIRST PERSON NARRATIVE

These leaves are feverish,
agitated by my clamber
and I'm hidden inside the tree,
the depth of its dark a comforting thing –
trying not to look at the lit shape of house
where he might take hours
to understand he doesn't hear me
moving between rooms
and eventually his search will take him to the garden
where I will have already felt
for wide circumference,
healthy limb, (just my luck to tie
to something rotted, unreliable)
and whatever sound I make he does not hear it,
only later sees the branch
capable of bearing a fast,
dropped, calamitous weight.

*

Wisp, thought of.
Came when we had
forgotten you were wanted.
Brought joy, brought storms.
Tethered, you persisted.
Then a formation of clouds.
Your skin, mottling.
This lack, aperture,
we snatch at it.

*

See how he touches
the fabric at my waist,
the way it gathers
and he feels the size of me, the delicacy
as I whisper things
to make him throw back his head
and laugh at the new sky above us
with everyone watching,
wanting us to carry on
with this intoxicating
notion of promise.
Look at us dancing.
We know nothing.
We knew nothing at all.

FACES IN A FACE

LINA MERUANE
tr. ANDREA ROSENBERG

'Y todo esto es mío y no lo es,
y parezco judía y no lo parezco.'

'So everything is mine and yet it isn't,
and I look Jewish and I don't.'
Margo Glantz, *Las genealogías* (The Family Tree)

FACES IN MY FACE

It's dawn, it's October, it's Berlin's Tegel Airport, and I'm en route again
to some European city. I've got a cup of black coffee balanced in one hand
while the other is pulling a suitcase, and since there's no escalator, I get
into the lift. Riding up with me is a couple dressed for vacation. Ripped
jeans, polo shirts, tennis shoes, two massive suitcases. He's got a pirate
bandana tied around his head. I'm silent as the three of us ascend. The
pirate turns to me and, faintly smiling, asks if I'm Hebrew. *You are Hebrew,*
he says, like that, in English, taking it for granted that I am. An odd way
of asking if I'm Jewish or if I'm Israeli, conflating religious and national
identity with the language. *Hebrew?* I avoid the eyes of the pirate, who
must speak Hebrew himself. *Why?* I say, hearing the irritation in my tone,
my voice breaking out in hives. *Do I look like I am?* The pirate hesitates
a moment, the smile still plastered on his face as he listens to me say that
maybe my face looks Mediterranean. (But what does it mean to be or
look Mediterranean, I wonder now as I write?) I've spent years explaining that I'm not *French Italian Greek Egyptian Spanish Turkish,* that I'm
not even entirely Palestinian, however much, the one time I travelled to
Palestine, the trained eye of the Israeli security forces instantly detected
my Palestinian origins. *Of course, Mediterranean,* the pirate's girlfriend
says in a conciliatory tone, attempting to rescue him from his shipwreck.
But he smiles with absolute confidence and states it's not just my face. *We
Hebrews are very lazy,* he says, *you can spot us because instead of climbing stairs
we take the lift. Like you,* he says, his teeth gleaming triumphantly. Like me,
I think, looking down at the coffee now burning in my left hand. My
right is holding my suitcase, and a backpack is slung precariously over my
shoulder. The hot coffee and my difficulty finding firm footing on *stairs
hands shoulders suitcase and backpack.* And I'm tempted to explain that that's
why I'm in this elevator. But the doors open and I realise that's not the
answer and I go ahead and tell them I'm not Israeli or Jewish but actually
Palestinian, or of Palestinian descent, which in their eyes must be pretty
much the same thing.

It wasn't the first time an Israeli had identified me as a Jew, I told
myself as I studied my face in the airport bathroom mirror and thought
back to the woman who'd once come up to me at a bus stop in Jerusalem
to ask me the time in a language I didn't recognise. I'd apologised, saying
in English that I didn't speak Hebrew or Arabic. The woman rebuked me
in a tongue I then understood, raising her voice to exclaim one of the few
words I knew in Hebrew. *Arabic! Arabic! Who's speaking Arabic here?* How
dare I think she might be an Arab? But she was the one who'd spoken to
me, and in Hebrew, I thought; she'd assumed she was speaking to an Israeli.

The two pirates were still outside, waiting at the gate for the Turkish
flight to Tel Aviv. The same flight I'd board a few weeks later, with
another cup of boiling coffee in my hand and the same suitcase in
the other.

ERASING A FINGERPRINT

How many faces are hidden in a face?

I scrubbed my face in that airport bathroom, trying to erase it. Erase from it what was not my own. For a moment I thought that maybe I shouldn't erase it entirely — every face is unique, a fingerprint. But then I remembered that fingerprints wear down over time; if they can disappear from your fingers, a face can certainly be washed away too.

VARIATIONS ON THE SAME

I close my eyes the night before my return to Palestine, before what will be my *real* return if they let me in. And though I was sure I'd washed off my Jewish face, beneath the surface markers of it have reappeared. It is because of those markers that so many people have been marginalised — the shape of their faces, the complexion of their skin, the colour of their eyes, the line of their eyelids, the thickness of their brows. The high, flat cheekbones. The hooked nose. The untrustworthy lips of an entire people, suspected just for bearing a particular face. Rejected. I shake my head back and forth as I think about the bun I plan to use to hide my curls, the clothes I'll wear to throw them off the scent. And the answers to a million potential questions I wasn't ready for last time. I start practising them with my imaginary interrogator. Chilean, yes. US resident, yes. University professor, yes. Writer, what kind of writer? Journalist? Palestinian? And have you ever been to Israel, yes, I say, hearing my voice leap from one neuron to the next, my voice sparking in the middle of the synapse. Up to that point, I can't attempt to hide the real answers because they're recorded in my virtual biography. But I also practise fake answers, the cold blood of falsehood or omission, because I've learned that Palestinians must never confess, that one piece of their peaceful resistance is the truncated answer or the non-answer or, better yet, the fake answer, and I know that in order to lie or leave things out I have to train myself to look straight ahead without lowering my eyes and without ever smiling at the agent. I can say I'm on vacation, say I'm staying at the home of my friend Maurice, an academic I met at a conference a couple of months back. I cannot say that Maurice is a Palestinian born in exile who then returned, that he's married to a Palestinian. Cannot say that Maurice has written an essay about my book on Palestine. Cannot say that in that book I criticised Israeli policies. Nor that I've given talks, sat for interviews, written a poem of denunciation. Nor that I'll be staying not in Ramallah but instead at the Jerusalem Hotel next to the Wailing Wall. Nor that I'm planning to visit resistance projects in the West Bank, or that I'll be taking the opportunity to visit my aunts, from whom I haven't heard since I met them at their home in Beit Jala five or maybe six years ago. That house made of stone, firmly rooted on a hill. But I cannot talk about their home or speak their names without getting us all in trouble. Again an empty sentence, and again and again another one that puts them off the track, and variations on the same until fatigue overcomes me and the cock crows.

ISRAELI FACE

They don't ask me one question at the airport. Not a single one. There must be some mistake; I keep waiting. My legs are reluctant to move on, my body wants to stop in the boarding area and demand those questions I've prepared for. My lungs are swollen with answers and I'm about to burst when the open smile of the flight attendant deflates me: this Turkish airliner has a layover in Istanbul and it's the next plane that will be taking me to Tel Aviv. And if they don't question me there, they definitely will in Ben Gurion. I land once and board another plane and land again and only in Tel Aviv am I faced with an immigration agent. I hand over my passport and wait for the official to examine the stamp-filled pages. The man flips briefly through my passport and then raises his tired eyes and asks me my father's name. *Does he live in Chile?* My veins burn with adrenaline. I brace myself for the interrogation that's coming and then doesn't come. *Go ahead*, he tells me, and I wonder, dejected, if he has recognised my Israeli face.

CHILEAN PASSPORTS

Following a map of Ramallah, my Greek companion and I reach the bus station flanked by a coffee shop with a round green logo called Stars & Bucks that is and yet is not an American coffee shop. The street seems packed with people, women either bareheaded or swathed in long dresses, and men, especially merchants, taxi drivers, passersby, minibus drivers shouting at the top of their lungs. Every time we ask which of the yolk-yellow minibuses is going to Bethlehem, we're given different instructions; the drivers we ask are always on their way to other towns. Somebody leads us to the mall and points us toward a lift, and at the top we find minibuses to our destination. We sit in the back row, in the two remaining seats next to a youngish Arab man, and all of us head out into the light, toward the highway, toward the south. We have half an hour ahead of us, my companion and I. We are talking about the road we are travelling on, who it belongs to. We speculate about what Bethlehem will be like, how long it will take us to walk around it before we split up.

It is then that the Arab man pipes up and asks where we're from. From Greece, says the Greek activist. From Chile, say I, the Chilean, and the Palestinian face of the Arab man lights up. *I'm a little bit Chilean too*, he says, *as of today*, he continues, in a Palestinian-inflected English. And opening his backpack he produces a bright burgundy passport with gold lettering and the crest with its condor and huemul, also in gold, and an ID card they've sent him from Santiago. They are the same two documents that I'm carrying in my own backpack. A quick exchange of documents, my fingers racing through the pages until I reach his identity: the passport claims that the Chilean man is Nicola Jadalah Tit, but the Palestinian man tells me he actually has four given names, Nicola Antón Hanna Khalil, followed by his father's surname, Tit, or Alteet, meaning *the Tit family*. In Chile they've given him his mother's last name. And though I want to ask how it is that the Civil Registry has screwed up and turned him into two people, how they've managed to mix up his last names even now, with the twenty-first century well under way, with computers and scanners and a bureaucracy full of educated people, another question is vibrating in my inner ear.

Tit. Alteet. Eltit?

Yes, he says in English, a proud *yes*. Alteet and Eltit are the same name with pronoun attached. And his Chilean Eltit relatives are so close to his father that they come to visit every summer with their burgundy passports. He says this in English because Nicola's Spanish is about as good as my Arabic, two or three polite words. But I kept going back to that last name, Eltit, because it is the name of the writer, a descendant of Beit Jala, who was my mentor years back, in my twenties. Given her name, I sometimes joked that our families had probably been neighbours, that maybe we even had relatives in common. Maybe we were distant cousins without knowing it. And Diamela Eltit would laugh at this idea, agreeing that it might be true: Beit Jala was such a tiny place during the years of the great migration that there'd been no need to name the streets or

number the houses. *Do you know who Diamela Eltit is?*, I ask him enthusias-
tically, feeling a rush of envy at the Eltits, whose last name is still around
while mine has disappeared from the face of Palestine. There aren't any
Meruanes left, I think to myself, just those aunts who carry my blood or
I carry theirs but who cares who the blood belongs to, I remind myself,
it's all family ties.

Diamila, he slowly repeats, interrupting my thoughts as he dusts off his
memory. *No, no Diamila*. He bites his lip and shakes his head swathed in
its thick black hair and beard. He doesn't know who Diamela is, he didn't
know there was such an important Chilean writer with his last name,
and he smiles, his eyes, black too, narrowing, embarrassed that he doesn't
know her, that he's never heard her name before. He promises to ask his
father, who'll definitely know. Because his father lived in Chile for
a number of years, whereas he's never set foot there.

A GIRL FROM BEIT JALA

Nicola doesn't know that so many Beit Jalans live in Chile, that there are
probably more of them in my country than in his, although *country* isn't
the word so I repeat, more Beit Jalans in my land than in yours. There
are more Palestinians living in Chile than in any other place outside of
Palestine and the Arab world, I say, they migrated in great numbers in
the early twentieth century, when the Ottoman Empire was having some
trouble and young Arabs, Christian Arabs especially, were being sent to
war as cannon fodder... The Turks suspected Christian Palestinians of
being allied with the Europeans, or loyal to the Europeans, because of
their religion. So it was mostly Christians, mostly Eastern Orthodox, who
came from Bethlehem and Beit Sahour and Beit Jala, I add, showing off
my recently acquired historical knowledge. And why would they all go to
Chile, right? Nobody knows! Nobody I've asked, anyway. It's like a legend
— everybody has a story. But it's probably very simple: one Palestinian
brought another Palestinian, a sibling, a sister, and because they were able
to live a better life, they stayed. Nicola shakes his head in silent disbelief
and then smiles awkwardly because what does he know about Chile
other than that his father spent some years of his youth there? Nicola's
not even familiar with Chile Square, which is on the bus route to Beit
Jala; he hasn't paid attention to the fact that there is also a Chile School
in his own town. I wonder what that square and that school are known
as to locals, in Arabic, but I insist to him that there *is* a square called
Chile — I got off there when I last visited your town, I took a picture
of myself under a blue marker probably funded by my own Chilestinians,
my oldest Palestinian aunt who is and is not Meruane lives around the
block — but Nicola raises his bushy eyebrows like he's shrugging his
shoulders and, changing the subject, says to me, *You look so much like a girl
from Beit Jala*. And he says it isn't just my face, my hair, but also the way
I laugh, that easy laugh, and the way I use my hands when I talk.

UNCERTAINTY

Greece, which is what I've started calling her, a name to which she has
politely acquiesced, will be going to Jerusalem on one bus, and I'll head
to Beit Jala on another, to look for my aunts. Nicola will be picked up by
his father: he speaks to him on the phone while Greece and I say goodbye, and in the midst of his Arabic sentences behind me I catch the word
Chile. Chile. Every so often my country garbed in that language I cannot
penetrate. Nicola's father, Antón, has never returned to Chile, and he now
wants to meet me, wants to be the one to take me to Beit Jala and drop me

off in Chile Square next to my aunts' house. And though it may not be a good idea to get into a car with not one stranger but two, I say goodbye to Greece, whose bus is already leaving, and walk with Nicola to the corner where he and his father have arranged to meet. We climb into a wheezing jalopy and the man, now elderly, has me sit in front so he can talk to me in a Chilean Spanish sprinkled with the occasional French word and coloured by a Palestinian accent. He speaks quickly because Beit Jala is so close that we won't have much time. He comes to a stop a few minutes later; we've arrived at Chile Square. *¿Dónde viven tus tías?* Over there, I say, pointing uncertainly at a little side street where I think they live. But maybe it's the other street. Now I'm not so sure. *¿Y a qué horas te esperan?* he asks, but nobody is expecting me. *¿Y cómo dijiste que era el nombre?* And I repeat my aunts' last name, both of their first names, *Maryam, Nuha.* I don't know them, he says suspiciously, and he looks back at his son and they exchange ideas and Antón tells me, Look, I don't know them but I know a few members of the family and they should know, but it's lunchtime now and I've made some artichokes stuffed with meat and, what's the word — he doubts his Spanish again — *¡arroz!* Come eat with us and afterwards I promise I'll help you find them. I immediately think about Palestinian hospitality, about the four courses that could eat up the little time I have for this visit, but I figure I'm going to need help in this land that is both familiar and unknown, so I accept, letting the father know in Spanish and the son in English that I won't be able to stay long. With that settled, the father starts the ancient engine and we head toward the Tits' home at the top of a hill.

CITIZENS OF THE WORLD

Nicola would tell me afterwards, months later in our written correspondence, that his father Antón hadn't just lived in Chile but also in *France Algeria Jordan Brazil*, and that he'd spent summers in *Turkey Lebanon Egypt Syria Libya Cyprus Bulgaria Monte Carlo Nice*, back when it was still easy to travel. It was returning home that turned out to be difficult. Antón was teaching in Algeria with his sister when she decided to get married. It was 1967, the year of a bloody war that lasted just six days but forever changed, yet again, the fate of Palestinians. It was 1967 and they didn't let brother or sister across the border. 1967. The same year my grandfather — already an adult, already married, already the father of five adult children, already a citizen of the Republic of Chile — tried in vain to visit his home in Palestine for the first time. Young Antón, too, was unable to enter and went instead to Chile, where his uncles lived and worked. *They used to work in textile, in bunnies iris with recollita*, Nicola wrote in an email, and I translated to myself while looking at a map of a neighbourhood in downtown Santiago I don't know that well, Buenos Aires Street, I read at the tip of my fingernail, and, off to one side, Recoleta. *He lived near fatronato, and his uncle used to live in rio dejunaro*, which was Patronato and Rio de Janeiro, *and bunnes aries*, Buenos Aires, *and he used to work in this area.* He'd worked with the Eltit uncles in that neighbourhood crisscrossed by streets named after cities, and eventually opened his own clothing store. Of all the places he knew, Chile was where Antón had lived the longest, almost seven years, and he'd become a citizen by the time he was forced to return by his father, the elder Tit or Alteet, who'd forbidden him to live in a foreign country past his thirties. He was expected to return to marry a Palestinian woman and have Palestinian children, so that's what Antón had done just before the Chilean coup d'état in 1973.

LAST NAME AS LABYRINTH

We drive up and down various streets but my aunts aren't where I left
them five years earlier. The stone houses all look alike. The steep street
blurs together with the photo I remember taking, but my phone is now
dead so I can't retrieve old pictures and compare them to what I'm seeing
on the narrow streets. I ring a doorbell. A young man appears, shirtless,
seemingly roused from a nap, and tells me he doesn't know the Abu
Awad sisters I'm asking about. So we go around and around some more
but the house from my memory has disappeared. Antón tells me not to
worry. He knows a number of Abu Awads. We'll go to their houses and
ask about my aunts, the only surviving aunts that carry my last name in
Beit Jala, their Meruane very far behind or buried alive under the weight
of other Arab names. These aunts who are descended from my grandfather's elder sister. Maryam is the eldest sister, followed by Nuha, or that's
what I understood the only time I met them. *Am I certain this is their last
name?* But my certainty is gone, laid low by my faulty recollection. We
drive around some more in that old car with Nicola in the backseat, and
we come to another stone house with several doors, front side rear, and
we knock on all of them until a young woman appears, three children
hanging from different parts of her body, and they talk while she eyes
me, curious, and I return her gaze, knowing she must be my distant
cousin. I see that she is nodding but then she shakes her head and looks
at me again and I at her, searching for a resemblance I don't find. I see that
Antón is also nodding slightly and turning around and telling me that
my aunt or our aunt is dead. As if an aunt could never die, as if five years
wasn't enough time for death to happen, as if dying itself wasn't possible,
I insist that she must be mistaken, it must be another Abu Awad, another
aunt of hers, her aunt but not mine, or mine too but not the one I'm looking for. I start describing the short, thick-waisted woman with cropped
black hair and deep wrinkles, she was in Chile years ago, she speaks some
Spanish, choosing verbs in the present tense of existence, rejecting the
past, even though in the past she'd hoped we would see each other again
in the future. And she has a younger sister. Taller, slimmer, I remember
her dressed in an orange cardigan while her elder sister was dressed in
black. Antón translates, and she keeps nodding, it's her, definitely her,
she died just a few months back from brain cancer.

DEATH MASK

The house seems different to me now that I've found it again. Different
people. Maryam's brother lives on the second floor, where I've never
been: a brother I've never seen before, with a wife. We sit in the kitchen
where the wife who speaks bits of broken Spanish is cooking dinner. He,
who speaks only Arabic, repeats my name over and over as if he needs to
repeat it in order to memorise it, *Leena, Leena,* the ees stretched out and
my name turned Arabic in his mouth. He offers the girl from Beit Jala
that I now am oranges that he peels himself and coffee that he's made for
me. Unable to talk to each other, we use gestures, hands moving in the air,
eyelids fluttering. And I know they telephone the other sisters. Others,
I think, how many? And here comes Lucía, she arrives first and smiles
and hugs me and looks at me intently while I wonder what she sees, who
she is seeing, but she doesn't say. And then Nuha, who looks at me a
moment, recognises me the next, and embraces me. Her slim body shakes
as she sobs against my collarbone. I'd like to weep along with her but I'm
so delighted to see her, delighted to have found her again, alive, delighted
to be meeting these other members of my family I've never heard of. And

maybe that's why I wish Nuha would stop doing what she's doing now. Lacking the words to describe her sorrow, she hands me her telephone and plays a video of Maryam in her final days. Her dead sister is still alive, sitting in a chair talking to somebody's kid. Her wrinkled face swollen from medications has become strangely unwrinkled. An unrecognisable Maryam. Illness has changed her face, buried her name and placed a terrible mask on top of it. The mask she wore to her grave.

ANNIE ERNAUX   INTERVIEW

In 1999, living in France for the first time, I picked up a copy of *Passion simple* by Annie Ernaux at the Fnac. My French wasn't great, but the vocabulary was simple, as was the subject: one woman's obsession with her Russian lover. 'From September last year,' she writes, 'I did nothing else but wait for a man: for him to call me and come round to my place.' Entire days slip by in this heightened state: the cycle of waiting, then finally hearing from him, or seeing him, then the emptiness again, followed by the immediate hunger to repeat the experience. It taught me so much about the unfulfilment of fulfilment. I loved how spare and almost unemotional the prose was, all while evoking this most emotion-ridden of experiences, and in time, reading her other work, I would come to understand that this *écriture plate*, or flat writing, was one of its strongest, most unique attributes. From books like *La place* (A Man's Place, 1983, for which she won France's prestigious Prix Renaudot) or *Une femme* (A Woman's Story, 1988), about the deaths, respectively, of Ernaux's father and mother, to *Les Années* (2008), recently published in English, translated by Alison L. Strayer, as *The Years*, Ernaux demonstrates a striking ability to take the most wrenching of experiences and render them unflinchingly, without moral judgment.

Ernaux was born in 1940 in Normandy to a working-class family; her parents worked in a factory and later ran a small café and shop. This background informs all of Ernaux's work, from her early anti-novels *Les Armoires vides* (Cleaned Out, 1974) and *Ce qu'ils disent ou rien* (1977) to her later masterpieces *L'événement* (Happening, 2000), about an illegal abortion, or *Mémoire de fille* (2016), which takes place during the summer of 1958, when she worked as a counsellor at a summer camp in Normandy, and explores the shame she felt following her first sexual experience with another counsellor there.[1] Elizabeth Bowen once described herself as a writer 'for whom places loomed large'; this is also true of Ernaux, for whom the past is a place, class is a place, photographs are places, writing is a place. Perhaps this is because of the way she has moved between classes, as she described to Michelle Porte in a documentary made about her work: 'My parents lived in fear of "falling back on factory work", as they put it, but it was much greater, a much older, more visceral fear, a certainty of their limitations. I passed into a world that doesn't have the same ethos, the same ways of being, or thinking. This disruption remains within me, even on a physical level. There are situations where I feel... No, it's not timidity, or discomfort. But place. As if I weren't in the right place... The place where none of this exists is writing. Writing is a place, an immaterial place.'

So, to place what you are about to read: we sat in Ernaux's beautiful, airy house in the *ville nouvelle* of Cergy, a half-hour's drive outside of Paris. She perched on a blue velvet settee; at one point her 15-year-old granddaughter came in to say hello. The house, where she has lived for forty years, and written all but the first two of her books, stayed remarkably cool, in spite of the heatwave; it opened out onto a veranda with a view of a green field and some young, graceful trees. The interview took place in French; any translation errors or infelicities are mine alone. It lasted almost two hours and has been condensed; in what I cut we talked, among other things, about my current pregnancy, her pregnancies, her grandchildren, and the American writers I urged her to read (Chris Kraus and Maggie Nelson). What I could not capture in transcription or translation is her laugh — this amazing lovely flirtatious laugh. I wish you could hear it.   LAUREN ELKIN

TWR It's amazing to be here in Cergy, as I'm such a fan not only of your *Journal du dehors* and *La vie extérieure* but of Eric Rohmer and the film he made here, *L'Ami de mon amie* (1987). Having grown up in the American suburbs, I'm really interested in the way both you and Rohmer write the *ville nouvelle*, transforming it from a *non-lieu*, in Marc Augé's term, into a *lieu*. Place is so important in your work — I wonder if you might say a bit about Cergy and the role it's played for you?

AE As you say, it's never been a *non-lieu* for me. For one thing it's a city that was conceived of on its own terms, rather than being an extension of a larger city; the concept is totally different. It has its own intense life. I came to it very early on, when it was just being built up, which was actually pretty destabilising because really we had no idea what it would become. It's only now, fifty years since its foundation, that we can begin to see. It has some of the characteristics of American suburbs, in that there are plenty of green spaces and detached houses, and it doesn't have that European city feeling of there being the historical centre in the middle and the suburbs all around. It's changed a lot since Rohmer filmed here in the mid-80s!

TWR I really identified with *Journal du dehors*, where you describe taking the train in and out of Paris, and the way that prompts you to relate to the city and to your town; having grown up on Long Island and eventually moving to New York City, most of my early adult life was a question of feeling caught between those two worlds, the suburb and the big city. I find that feeling of living between two worlds very interesting.

AE Yes, that's true, it's living between two worlds. Parisians — those who live intra-muros, in the arrondissements — have a very hazy relationship to the banlieues, they generally take a pretty negative view of them; they put Cergy in the same category as Saint Denis or somewhere like that, when really it's not the same thing at all.

TWR I've just been reading the interviews you gave for Michelle Porte's documentary [published as *Le Vrai lieu* (Real Places) in 2014], and you talk about another kind of separation, that of living this intellectual, creative life so far removed from the milieu where you were born and raised, in Normandy. What is this separation, and how is Cergy an answer to this problem of milieu?

AE As a class defector [*transfuge de classe*], I've

never felt comfortable in Paris. I prefer to be in a place which has no history, that is no History with a capital H, with all the signs of the past that you find in old cities, the marks of power, the ornate architecture — there's none of that here. Basically Cergy is a place that is very welcoming to people who've left their homes far behind. The provinces where they come from are very marked by social differences, and by the whole of the past — in the town where I grew up everyone knew who your parents were, who your grandparents were, et cetera. You couldn't escape it. Paris, for me, would have been the same thing all over again.

TWR Your work is often interested in the quotidian, in writing the everyday — for me you're part of a group of postwar French writers like Georges Perec, who was so committed to writing and memorialising places, or Michel de Certeau or Pierre Bourdieu, who analyse the practices of everyday life. How do you see yourself with regard to these writers?

AE Oh definitely, Bourdieu, Perec, they take me way back. I discovered Perec when I was 25, reading *Les Choses* (Things: A Story of the Sixties, 1965), which was a revelation for me. I had already written a novel which a couple of editors had turned down, so I had stopped writing and started having children. And somewhere in there I discovered Perec, and I thought — this is something completely new! I wanted to write something like that. I really envied him! Once I accidentally made reference to him while talking to a journalist, who told me 'That's not literature, it's sociology.'

TWR What!

AE Of course it was literature! So Perec prompted me to find a way to write a kind of real fiction [*une fiction réelle*], which would not only be real but also very contemporary, in the here and now. His voice was definitely one to follow. Then a bit later there was Pierre Bourdieu with *Les Héritiers* (1964), when I realised I was exactly the kind of student he was referring to: scholarship students who are not entirely at ease in the culture, who have to adapt themselves to their new surroundings. That's when I started to write *Les Armoires vides* [Ernaux's first published novel]. At the time I couldn't have called myself a class defector, that kind of language came later, but I would have called it a kind of wrenching away from my class of origin, the working class. I didn't come in contact with legitimate culture until I was at university, and I had to acquire it bit by bit. I turned my back on everything I had wanted when I was younger — I was very influenced, for example, by Virginia Woolf.

TWR   Does any of that live on in *Les Armoires vides*?
AE   Not at all, I put an end to it. Even though there's much to work with in Woolf's texts, certain sensations, certain visions — but you know at a certain point even she wrote that she needed another word than 'novel' to describe what she was doing.

TWR   She writes in a letter to her sister Vanessa Bell how ridiculous it was that the reviewer in the *Times* had praised her characters in *The Waves* when she meant to have none.
AE   She wasn't interested in the traditional psychology of character. That really struck me, and it's something that's continued to be true of my work.

TWR   So you would not consider yourself a novelist.
AE   No, that's a term that doesn't suit me at all. Even more so as we tend to call women writers 'novelists', while male writers get to be just 'writers'. And there are always more men being asked to write about literature than women in the book pages of *Le Monde* — in the collective unconscious 'writer' means 'man'. Or maybe that's just how it is in France.

TWR   I think it's like that in the US and UK as well. So are you in favour of the feminisation of language[2]? Do you refer to yourself as an *écrivaine*?
AE   Yes I do. At the beginning I didn't want to, but now it's more of a question of habit. I don't go so far as to use *écriture inclusive*[3] but it doesn't bother me.

TWR   Would you describe what you do as autobiography, or as essay-writing?
AE   Neither. I'm very interested in the idea of a genre-less text. But then you're taking the risk that others will endanger it by saying it's not literature if it isn't assigned a precise genre. But there are more and more texts like this — and many of these writers persist in calling them 'novels' even when it's clearly not what they've written, because novels sell. I've refused to do that.

TWR   In an essay you wrote about *Journal du dehors*, you said that it was an attempt to write in a '*je transpersonnel*'. What does that mean?
AE   What I mean by that is everything that could be opposed to the autobiographical *je*. In the *je* as I conceive of it, it's not an identity that aligns with me and my history, it's not a psychological *je*, it's a *je* that is marked by the communal experiences which many of us have known — the death of one's parents, the condition of women, illegal abortion. The epitome of this *je transpersonnel* is *The Years*, where the *je* completely disappears. For me the *je* is not an identity, but a place, marked by human experiences and human events. That is what I try to illuminate through my writing. I say *je transpersonnel* because it is not the individual, or the anecdotic, that interests me, but that which is shared, whether that be social, or even slightly in the order of the psychological, in the realm of reaction. That is how I may be sure that I'm bringing to light something that isn't reducible to a personal history. Essentially, I want to put myself at a distance, the greatest distance between what I've lived, who I am — it's about being able to distance yourself. It's an attitude, of course, and it took time to construct; my earliest books are very marked by affects. There are still affects later on, but you have to find a way to talk about affect without having it be attributable to the writer herself.

TWR   Does that come through in the 'flat writing' style people often talk about with regard to your work?
AE   Yes — flat because I wrote it that way, it came to me that way — it's more objective, distanced, factual.

TWR   When you say it comes to you that way, does that mean that you don't write a whole mess of a draft and then cross out everything that is too personal or affective?
AE   No. It's born of a certain approach to the blank page, which is perhaps easier in my position — it's very important to have changed classes, because I don't take writing as a given. I am between what Bourdieu would call the habitus — my class habitus, my first culture, my way of life in the working class, and literature, and what I experience as literature. In writing I'm always striving to resolve these two worlds, and the difficulty lies in trying to carry into literature something of my first culture.

TWR   It's very spatial, the way you describe it.
AE   Yes, as you say, it's very spatial, as if there were two different places that had to be brought together: the place I started from, which has a certain violence, and the world of literature. In a way, every time I write, I'm conquering something. Do you see what I mean?

TWR   Yes, completely. It's something you have to strive for; it isn't a given.
AE   It isn't a given.

TWR   There are a lot of blank spaces in your books — is that a visual translation of this spatial relationship to the act of writing and to writing itself?
AE   Yes. But not in all of my books — in *The Years* there aren't as many blanks.

TWR   But there is something interesting in the way you've laid the text out on the page.
AE   Yes — the spacing! For me it's fundamentally important to include this space. It's the site of the illegible, of difference — of rupture, of forms of rupture. Yes, it's a bit like that. But then it's not a space for me, but rather for the reader.

TWR   One of the most striking things for me about *The Years* is that it is one of the only books in your entire career where you use the third person. How did you conceive of this voice? What happened to the *je* which is so important in your other books?
AE   It evolved to the point of disappearance in *The Years*, and also in my last book, *Mémoire de fille*, which is in two different and very distinct voices, the first and the third. *Je* for the woman who writes, and *elle* for the person I'm describing, the young woman of 1958.

TWR   Was *The Years* the first time you wrote in the third person?
AE   Yes.

TWR   How did that feel? I can't write at all in the third person, it always feels so artificial!
AE   You may just need time! And in any case it's not necessarily an ideal. What happened to me is the opposite — after years of writing in *je*, now I can no longer write in the first person.

TWR   Why?
AE   I don't know. I just feel it the same way I felt I had to write in *je* — as a necessity.

TWR   Is this *elle* perhaps just another, prismatic way of writing *je*? A way of turning *je* on its side?
AE   There is a lot of *je* in *elle*, it's not an invented *elle*, it's *elle/je* — but *elle* for short. Everything *elle* does is *je*. *Je* has just become impossible for me, not just grammatically.

TWR   It's another way of putting distance between yourself and the page.
AE   Yes, an even greater distance. But it makes it easier for me to speak, to write. I think I could not have written about everything that happened to the young woman of 1958 in *Mémoire de fille* if I had written it in the first person. It's really the *elle* that liberated me.

TWR   In *Le Vrai lieu* you talk about the ways in which society speaks through the writers it produces, and at the conclusion of *The Years* you offer the reader a way of approaching the text:

It will be a slippery narrative composed in an unremitting continuous tense, absolute, devouring the present as it goes, all the way to the final image of a life. An outpouring, but suspended at regular intervals by photos and scenes from films that capture the successive body shapes and social positions of her being — freeze-frames on memories, and at the same time reports on the development of her existence, the things that have made it singular, not because of the nature of the elements of her life, whether external (social trajectory, profession) or internal (thoughts and aspirations, the desire to write), but because of their combinations, each unique unto itself. To this 'incessantly not-she' of photos will correspond, in mirror image, the 'she' of writing.
There is no 'I' in what she views as a sort of impersonal autobiography. There is only 'one' and 'we', as if now it were her turn to tell the story of the time-before.

With that in mind I wanted to talk a bit more about this question of impersonal or collective autobiography. Women who write about their own lives are so often accused of narcissism, of navel-gazing, and the collective autobiography seems to me a more honest way of addressing the relationship between the I, the we, and the world that produced us, that speaks through us, and continually shapes and reshapes us.

AE   Yes exactly. At the beginning I had no intention of writing a collective autobiography. All the steps I took are inscribed within the text. What I wanted was to write the story of a woman who had lived through an era, but I almost wanted for her to not be there, and I didn't know how to do this — if I had taken her out completely it would have been a history book, there needed to be a consciousness inside the book. So I began accumulating images and memories which were at the same time personal and impersonal, as well as movies, books, memories, lyrics, without attributing them to anyone. I began with the time when I arrived in the world — I have no real memories of the world itself, but just afterwards. So the book became about this world of before — how we come to be aware of it. I wasn't writing about myself, but through narratives, through our ways of knowing, through the ways in which we encounter the world. It's not psychological, it's more about circumstances, family meals. It came to me right away that it wasn't about a particularly personal experience, but about this history of France, and this history of the country people, workers, the olden days. And then I had to find a way to continue, so I looked at old photographs, like my baby photo, but still, nothing happened, there was no one there. I don't know how I had the idea to use a [later] photograph, but I found this photograph of the little girl by the seaside, which is me of course, and I described this photo, and as I did, I realised I had to make a choice: was I going to write *je* or *elle*.

TWR   It was the photograph that prompted you to decide.

AE   I don't have my drafts here anymore, they're at the Bibliothèque nationale, but I know that for part of it I was using *je* as if I were the narrator, and I describe this photograph as a narrator, as the voice who writes. Then I put the book down for a while, and when I picked it back up again I started writing in *elle*, and after that I stopped using the *je* altogether as I plunged back into my memories of the 1950s. Then I was able to describe the world I grew up in — radio shows, advertisements, all sorts of memories. I wrote about the ruins after the war, because of course I was in Normandy,

as well as the phenomenal joy after the Liberation. I wanted my individual memories to serve as a collective memory. But there's no real difference, because the memory of particular events — my first circus, my first Tour de France — are collective memories, of which I retain an individual memory. I wanted very simply to make use of them to capture this epoch. It's not the archival work of a historian, who wouldn't have written in the first person either, or used his own memories. Whereas I use almost exclusively my own memories throughout the book. Collective memory is, in the end, how I lived, how everyone lived, how that way of life is within me.

TWR   It's very effective.

AE   I really wanted to write it like this but I was worried my editor wouldn't take it. I was worried it wouldn't be legible or comprehensible, I worried I'd made some kind of purely avant-garde, illegible text. And I thought oh well, I don't care, I'm going to write it how I want. And then [after it was published] I read articles where the critics said 'Ernaux has really done something different this time!' It seemed this kind of total decentring of the self had produced something worthwhile.

TWR   You give enough for the reader to go on to make sense of the text — in the *elle* sections, the descriptions of photos, and the little reading guide you slip in at the end.

AE   Even as I was writing I felt a form of illegitimacy, writing this kind of historical fresco as a woman. As if on some level I wasn't authorised to do it, to write this history through a woman's consciousness. But I have to admit, in France at least, no one contested me. So I was right to do it.

TWR   Did you write it chronologically?

AE   Yes, that was very important to me, to follow the course of time. It's a way of dominating it, of dominating history, by writing it. I absolutely cannot write out of order. I've always been that way, it was the same with *Mémoire de fille*, I can't write from a place of disorder. That doesn't mean I don't take notes, but the notes aren't written through. I call the notes I make 'civilisation notes', where I write down things I want to use in the future, but I don't write them through. For me, to write things through I have to relive time — relive time, perhaps to live it twice.

TWR   Or to give it form.
AE   Chronology has always fascinated me.

TWR   In *Écrire la vie* [the edition of her collected major works, published by Gallimard] your books are presented in chronological order, but not in the order in which you wrote them.
AE   In the end I didn't care for that. I would have preferred they be placed in order of composition.

TWR   So there's a chronology that takes precedence over another.
AE   What's more interesting than life is writing. Well, they're both interesting, but when you write a book, the writing of it is more important.

TWR   In the Anglophone world they're just discovering autofiction, as practiced by writers like Sheila Heti, Ben Lerner, or Jenny Offill.
AE   They're a little late!

TWR   I like its hybridity, its blur, the difficulty of pinning down what kind of text we have in front of us. So it's very much been on my mind as I reread your work this time around. I know that your books are often classified this way in France, but I know it's a label that you're not comfortable with.
AE   Right, because all the same there is a definition of autofiction — it's that there is no *pacte de vérité* [guarantee of truth], whereas in what I write there *is* a *pacte de vérité*. For example, take the photographs in *The Years*. People sometimes ask me if they're real photographs. They aren't invented, they exist, and everything I say about them is true. Whereas in autofiction there's the possibility of inventing the self. In general, autofictional books are published as novels. I never wanted my work to be associated with that movement.

TWR   But even in non-fiction, where there is an autobiographical pact, we know that the I who writes and the I on the page are not reducible to the same person, it's a narrator who is other than ourselves. Where I think it's possible for your work to be read as autofiction — and again this is just my reading of it — is in the space you were talking about before, between you and the text. That space opens up a distance which creates the possibility of autofiction, from the other direction, and more radically, I think: to upset what we think of as the truth in fiction is expected; to do it from non-fiction, or to refuse to class it as fiction, is not.

AE   It's completely possible. Detractors say that that memory isn't reliable, so it's all fiction anyway, but what matters is the question of intentionality. I wouldn't write a book like *Mémoire de fille* with the intention of changing anything; the book is a kind of research. Books that we call, in scare quotes, 'autobiographical' are explorations of something that took place, and the intention is to discover the truth of it. I'm not saying I manage this in the end, but what counts is the path towards truth, to look closer every time. In *Mémoire de fille* I was asking myself why I was in bed with that boy. It's a real question! Why didn't I get up? But I didn't.

TWR   I wanted to ask you about Virginia Woolf again, about a quote from her journal while she was trying to write her novel-essay *The Pargiters*, which she would eventually split into a novel and a work of non-fiction, *The Years* and *Three Guineas*.
AE   I have to interrupt you there! I had no idea while I was writing it that I'd stolen the title from Virginia Woolf! I didn't mean to!

TWR   Well what's really funny is that you managed to do in *The Years* what she wanted to do in *The Pargiters*, but failed! When she was planning it out, she wrote in her journal that 'it's to take in everything, sex, education, life &c.' It reminds me of that moment in *The Years* where the woman you describe has a kind of epiphany that brings her in tune with the entirety of existence:

> The tiny moment of the past grows and opens onto a horizon, at once mobile and uniform in tone, of one or several years. Then, in a state of profound, almost dazzling satisfaction, she finds something that the image from personal memory doesn't give her on its own: a kind of vast collective sensation that takes her consciousness, her entire being, into itself. She has the same feeling, alone in the car on the highway, of being *taken into* the indefinable whole of the world of now, from the closest to the most remote of things.

This seems incredibly close to Woolf's project: she wanted to write a really global, inclusive, genre-less book, and couldn't, but I think you've managed it in your version of *The Years*.
AE   That's very funny, I'm glad!

TWR   For Woolf it was difficult to find a way of combining the two types of writing — people and history.
AE   It took me a while to figure out how to do it. But it's good to have a big project like that. I'm in the midst of another vast project right now — it's not the same as *The Years*, you can't repeat yourself, but it's still pretty overwhelming. You can't reduce your ideas; when you have a big one you can't tell yourself you can't do it.

TWR   To come back to this question of the photographs, I love that so much of your writing flows from these ekphrastic descriptions of old photos.
AE   I wonder why, I've often wondered what the connection is. I wrote a book called *L'Autre fille* (The Other Daughter, 2011) — you know I had an older sister who died when she was six, whose existence I didn't learn of until I was almost 10 years old. There was a baby photo of her that they told me was me! So is it because of this that I have such a strong relationship to photography? You'd have to ask a psychoanalyst, I don't know. Then there's the fact that there were so few photos in the house, we didn't have a camera. Photographs are time, and they're death, because what's there in the photographs is essentially no longer there. The people in the photographs leave, or die, or we never see them again. I often go to Venice, and one time there was a kind of advertisement for the Biennale in a square and I amused myself by taking pictures of all the people who would come and sit on the bench next to it — adults, children, all sorts of people. I felt this irrepressible urge to take their picture, these people on this day that I'd never see again.

TWR   You describe *Journal du dehors* as an 'écriture photographique du réel', emphasising the photograph's ability to record, or observe, from a sociological perspective. But in *L'Usage de la photo* (The Use of the Photograph, with Marc Marie, 2005) you put yourself directly — or almost directly — into the frame, by photographing, with your lover, M., the clothing left on the floor after a moment of passion. It's such a great project, I love that the two of you thought to do that.
AE   That's a very quirky book, which was badly received — people were angry that I had written it with someone else. *L'événement* was also badly received, and now it's adapted for the theatre, and soon for the cinema — there's a young woman who came to see me, who wants to do it as a film.

TWR   It's a very good time for it — people are realising it's time to speak out about their experiences with abortion, to destigmatise it.
AE   Everything related to reproduction is such a problem. It's very visceral for men, and for society in general.

TWR   It's also very difficult to write — to be up to it stylistically without falling into the trap of the sentimental.
AE   Yes, that is very difficult.

TWR   But in *L'événement* you pull it off. It's a very hard book to read, it's 'writing like a knife', as you've said elsewhere.
AE   Exactly. When faced with this sort of subject, there is no good and there is no bad. There is just writing.

L. E.,
July 2018

1. *Ce qu'ils disent ou rien* and *Mémoire de fille* have yet to be translated into English; they might be translated as 'Their Way or No Way' and 'Portrait of the Artist as a Young Woman'.
2. French is a language that genders parts of speech to agree with the person to whom they refer; the word for 'writer' is écrivain (this could be a man or a woman but it is the masculine form) and the version used to refer specifically to a female writer is écrivaine. The debate over the feminisation of language has to do with whether it is more important to mark out difference, or to include women in universal (previously male) concepts.
3. A response to the ways in which the French language is gendered and exclusionary, which consists of introducing a median period plus the feminine and plural endings to words that would otherwise make it seem like there were only men involved — so écrivains becomes écrivain.e.s.

IMOGEN CASSELS

POETRY

OUR LADY OF THE SOIL
after Roger Caillois

That, summer, spent in churches,
I did not find *X* but he sought
to find me
                        where I watched him.

You'd make a great
candle he said, *I can see*
your muscles rushing through
the red fire red. That herbal acrid
look. Hot. Here hold this,
    madonna.

The fat flecked all along
the shop windows and crisped
gold like a relic. Pick your own.
God is an Italian; likes kitsch
and geometry. Victoriana.

I was the flower basket in the haywire cage.
Please, I said, I am trying to be
        a serious architect.
X said confess: He is like with my nerves
like a jazz kit. He is like with my heart
like blowing glass.
                X said *just love – whether it be fact*
                or fiction that love seemed nobler than
                its ultimate purpose. I didn't bother.

Mere spot – in sculpture, a cavity. I protested
we were figures and colours in space, other
than articulated sounds in time. No
loving without touch. No comment.

Yes I have been offered a modest fellowship
as a minor patron saint
                (of eyelashes)
in turn for re-burning, I
consider my options.

* * *

when the Passion occurred, or struck,
  I believe also that X could see
    with his round spectacles
      tiny pale buds in every pink
        and white, down the slopes
          of Calvary, Northern *fraises*,
          he never met. And the bugs watching
        from their tripods in the roses. This
      from diary number 109, our last, or
    the latest in exhaustive records.

Some date the concept of blue
  from this time, note, but its formal
    resistance to tattooing. Which as
      you all no emerges as our best chance
        of getting a fix – on anything. These
      days. Or light burns. The thought
    is only there if you can touch it,
  or find it waiting under new skin.

Portrait of the madonna as an early modern gentleman
  with a fresh sabre-cut from upstage left
to downstage right – his bone, the audience knows,
  would be exposed were it not for the just-dried
bloodline [cf. cocaine; synthesised crystal; salt rims
  on margaritas; frost rising into ice] on his cheek.

* * *

Victim impact statement from the Sea:
who said X stepped upon her one part further
than wanted or agreed; you trip-protestor,
you cold-shoulderer. It is very difficult
holding both of them. Something about
bladder-wrack, or guilt. A short bleed
of jellyfish in this morning's wash. How
he sank on the waves like a month or so
on tundra, sand, tinder. I have put X,
X, X, like touches into. Their yellow heads
in the long gulf between islands, like
the dead women's faces. Or isn't that
  a flower.

In between singing *One May morning* and the next folk
    X tells me, *My mother was a mantis*, and
    I can see her, a Tuscan psychedell. Her mother died
or drowned. She won't approach the font.

    Our Lady of the Soil. You must have caught the photos,
how every colour went awry in impossible ways –
    each foreign insect is a cloud of neon stars. Look
how his mother (the mantis) leans into the shoot,
    its bendy green. Girl knows how to pray
before a camera. Glass loves her. Glass loves her.
            She loves no man, only
                        mineral, the lure of space
                                    and nets.

    The downward pressure. Wrists
    you become snappable, curious.
    So is this translation I found
    myself asking. I'm very tired and
    very tired of metaphors. Well we
    are all really guilt, and fisheye lens.
    Touch me and commune with
    the disasters of others, I will
    receptacle. Ossify, ossify.

***

Maria: I thought you were *Mar*ia, or,
a lady of the moon. Instead a prickle thing,
bright acid. Your target object is
idle, a dreamer, chaste, vegetarian.

Clutter that poisons in kind –
lucky you, exoskeleton! (Somewhere your bony son
is being uncovered in his body's snoozy grotto.)
This is how you
            hypnotic trance.

Epaphrodites: she who is an invitation to love.
You're still a virgin if you kill him afterwards.
If you're lucky she looks like a cut-up flower.
Every mantis now is a sort of Mary, or lesser
    female saint. They look really good
    if you set them on fire. They're the agents
    on the ground, the leaf, the stem.

Portrait of the madonna as a young rhododendron,
    new prime and just skeletal. She is shaking very gently.
Green girl. Eden lapsing back in these small shadows.
    Don't let her trick.

Our Lady of Ash
Our Lady of Resin
Our Lady of Glass
Our Lady of Beetles

BETTINA SAMSON

Bettina Samson (b. 1978) is a French artist whose work delves into mathematics, meteorology and modern sculpture. In 'Kink (More Honour'd in the Breach)' (2015), a series of four head-sized sculptures made from terracotta grog, echoes of Brutalist architecture combine with the tangled limbs familiar from the work of Henry Moore. For 'Mètis & Metiista' (2013) Samson produced five glass borosilicate sculptures inspired by 'Klein bottles': non-orientable shapes first imagined by the German mathematician Felix Klein in 1882, and materialised in the 1990s by the British scientist and glass blower Alan Bennett. Like a Möbius strip, Klein bottles have a single surface, where inside becomes outside and vice versa. In Samson's rendering, the bottles allude to the human body: glass funnels become elbows, bases become bottoms, and coils become phalluses.

For her 2011 series 'L'éclat' ('Shine'), Samson replicated samples of iridium, a brittle silver-coloured element discovered in 1803 by the chemist Smithson Tennant. One of the rarest elements in the Earth's crust, iridium is implicated in the Alvarez hypothesis, which posits that the mass extinction of dinosaurs was caused by the impact of a large asteroid carrying the metal. Samson's 'L'éclat' sculptures are made from enamelled ceramic coated in platinum. Their forms are inspired by possible meteoric fragments found at the site of the Stony Tunguska River, Russia, in 1908, after the largest impact event in human history wiped out 2,000 square miles of forest. No conclusive evidence of a meteor was ever found, and the event remains shrouded in mystery.

PLATES

XVI	*Kink (More Honor'd in the Breach) I*, 2015
XVII	*Kink (More Honor'd in the Breach) II*, 2015
XVIII	*Kink (More Honor'd in the Breach) III*, 2015
XIX	*Kink (More Honor'd in the Breach) IV*, 2015
XX	*Mètis & Metiista I*, 2013
XXI	*Mètis & Metiista II*, 2013
XXII	*Mètis & Metiista V*, 2013
XXIII	*Mètis & Metiista II*, 2013
XXIV	*L'éclat 9*, 2011
XXV	*L'éclat 6*, 2011
XXVI	*L'éclat 12*, 2011

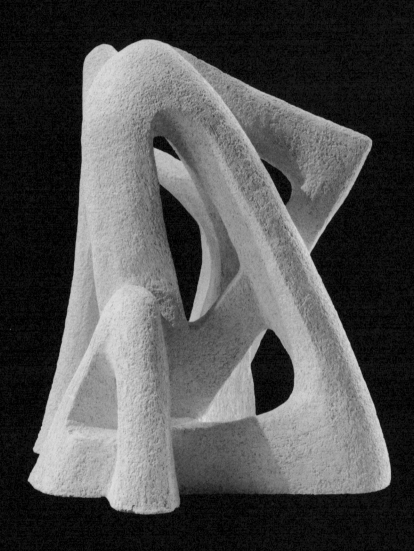

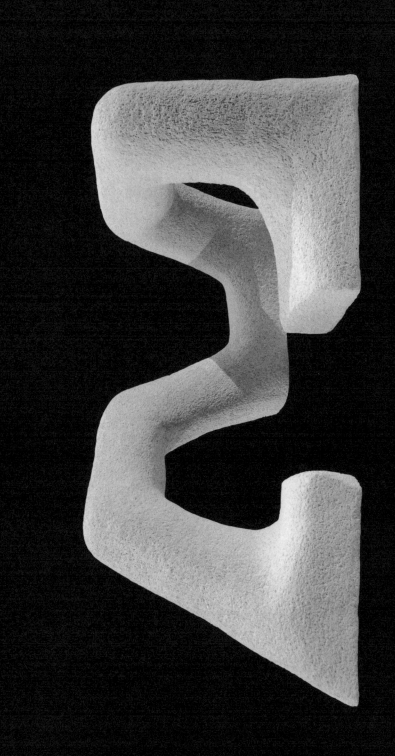

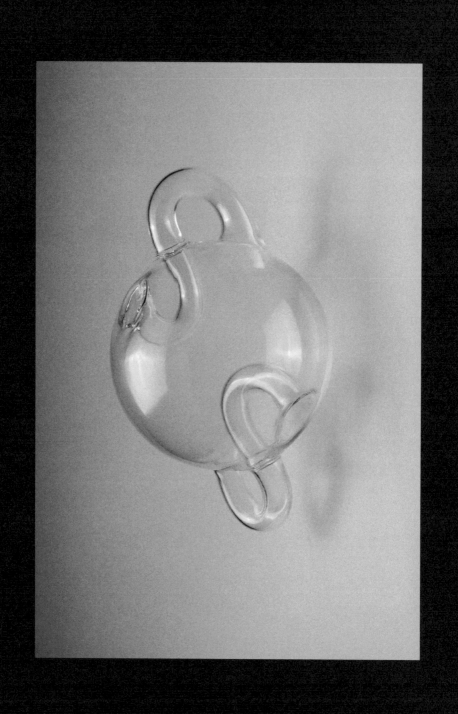

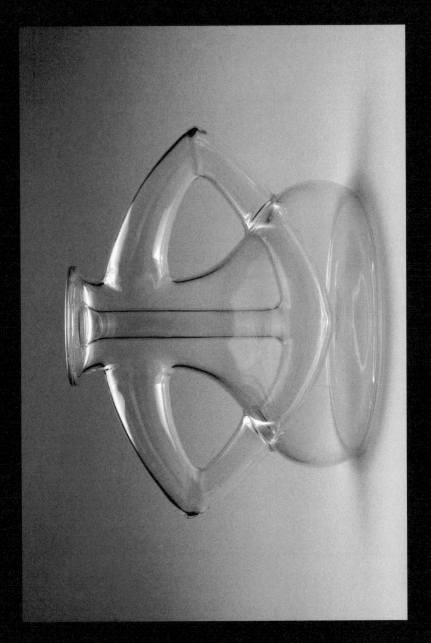

XXI

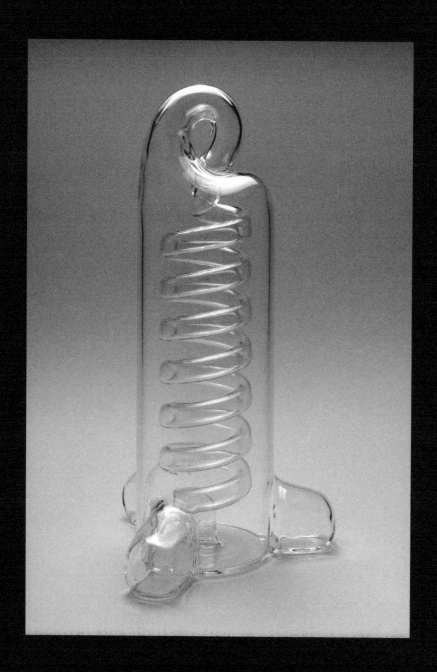

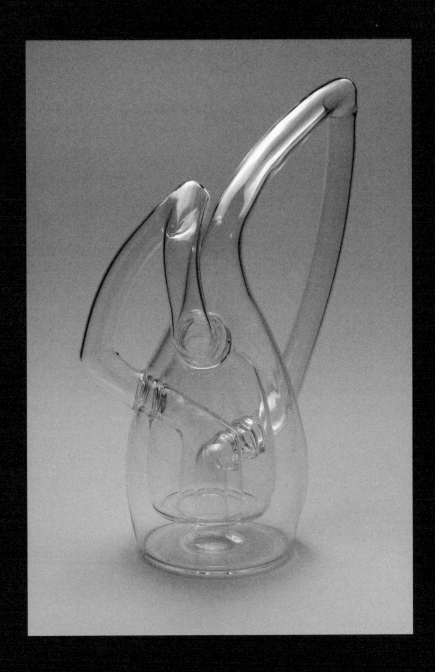

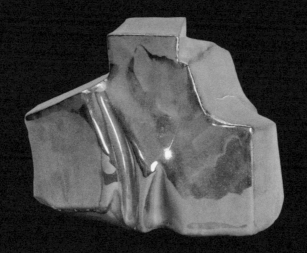

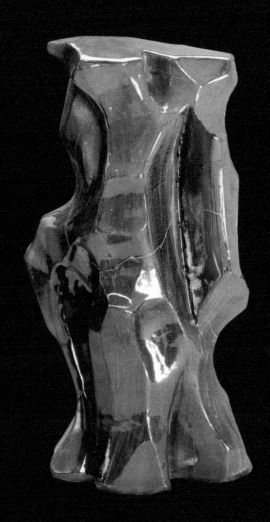

FRAGMENTS
NANAE AOYAMA
tr. POLLY BARTON

FICTION

His silhouette like an oversized cotton bud, my father waved to me, and so the day began.

He was standing there under the stretch of gingko trees lining Chuo-dori, a perfect parallel with the trunk reaching up beside him, the morning sun at his back.

In the open square outside the station, the beeping of the taxis, the revving of the bus engines and the voices of people calling to one other formed a dense layer-cake in the air, which was continuously pushed out into the cracks of sky between the buildings. Beside a coach parked alongside the gingkoes, a man in a blue safety vest called out a destination, read out a list of names, and the line of waiting passengers went filing inside.

Scattered around my waving father were various groups of women, hanging around, waiting for their coach to depart. The women were of different ages, shapes and sizes, but their laughter all sounded the same. There were a few children and young couples waiting too, faces either sleepy or mildly anxious-looking.

With his polo shirt buttoned right to the top, my father looked like a postage stamp stuck onto this scene. He could have easily been someone who just happened to be passing through.

As I navigated the clusters of women and made my way towards him, he brought his waving hand up onto his bald head and said, 'Blimey, it's hot.' His polo shirt clung tightly to his skinny torso, and the thighs peering out of his shorts were so puny that he looked like he'd only need the lightest of kicks to go toppling back onto the flowerbed behind him.

'It is,' I said, though it wasn't really that hot.

I had found myself here at Shinjuku station at seven o'clock on a Saturday morning because my father and I were going on a Pick-Your-Own-Cherries Tour.

But why me? I was still thinking to myself. It was supposed to be the five of us.

Because the tour was leaving so early, I'd gone back the previous evening to my parents' house in central Tokyo, only to discover that my baby niece Mariko, who was already there with my brother, had come down with a temperature. My mother, who seemed concerned by this development, announced that she'd stay at home to look after Mariko, and then my brother said he would too, and I was about to say the same thing when my mother said, in the voice she uses for delivering official decisions,

'So, just the two of you then.'

After calling the tour company to tell them that three people were cancelling, she turned away from the phone and said again, as if to confirm,

'So, just the two of you, okay.'

My father didn't respond. My brother, with Mariko sat on his knee, flashed me a grin.

'You should come!' I said. 'Can't you get Rikako to look after her?'

'Nah, Rikako's not back till next week. Mummy's taking a break, isn't she, Mariko?'

Mariko was drinking apple juice, her round face bright red.

'Not even for a day?'

'No, I really can't. She's off to Atami today, anyway. Listen, Mum: when Rikako comes back, don't mention that Mariko had a fever, okay?'

'Why not?'

'Because I'll get told off for not taking proper care of her, obviously.'

'You can't keep that kind of thing a secret from the child's own mother!' my mother replied. 'I've never heard anything like it!'

'It's true,' I said. 'Normal people don't go around hiding that kind of stuff. Besides, there's no need for you to stay at home, if Mum's here.'

'I can call them back, Eiji, if you want to go.'

'No, I don't. I couldn't sit there stuffing my face with cherries while Mariko's suffering at home.'

'You say that, but really you just can't be bothered. How about we swap, and I'll look after Mariko?'

'But you want to take photos, don't you? You should go,' said my brother.

'Yes, Kiriko should go,' my mother agreed.

'Why just me?!'

'It's not just you! Dad's going too. I don't see what the big deal is.'

'Yes, it's good to spend time alone with your father from time to time.'

As I was about to object, Mariko started to cough and spilled her juice across the table. My brother began flapping about and rubbing her back, and my mother ran out of the room to get a cloth. The juice travelled across the table top, slowly soaking into the corner of the evening paper spread out across its surface. My father, who was reading the paper, still said nothing at all.

This was the kind of thing that happened when Rikako left home.

Rikako was the self-composed, beautiful sort – so much so, in fact, that you had to wonder what she was doing with someone as immature as my brother – and it was very hard to imagine her with a temper. But she would from time to time, to borrow my brother's terminology, *hit the roof*. Having done exactly that last week, she had decided to take some time out, and had gone back to her parents' house in Takasaki. Usually when this happened, Rikako took Mariko with her, but this time, as if attempting to prove some kind of point, my brother had insisted that he do the honours. Then, leading a whinging Mariko by the hand, my brother had made the 10-minute journey straight to my parents' house.

Throughout the four years of their marriage, starting back when I was still living with my parents, my brother and his wife had done this a bunch of times. The only truly tense part was the first three or so days of their separation. After that danger period had passed, my brother would still return to my parents' house to sleep, but would talk with Rikako on the phone every night, laughing and joking. Sometimes their separation would last less than a week. One time, before Mariko was born, it had gone on for nearly two months.

This time, a phone conversation on day three had established that the leaving-home period would be limited to two weeks.

Having heard from my brother about Rikako's plans to go to the seaside town of Atami, my mother – heaven only knows what she was thinking – 'just so happened' to see the brochures for the Pick-Your-Own Cherries tour outside the travel agency on the way home from her part-time job, and went inside. She'd made the booking then and there, for five people: her, her husband, her son whose wife had run away and left him, his baby daughter, and her own daughter, who had specifically chosen a university on the far side of Kanagawa Prefecture to give herself a reason to live away from home.

Our tour group would assemble at Shinjuku at seven in the morning, board the tour bus, and drive to a cherry farm somewhere in Nagano where we could eat as many cherries as we wanted. In the afternoon we would take in the views along the Venus Line, the tourist route running through the Nagano highlands. As far as I could tell from the pamphlet, there were several options for the second half of the day, and the others sounded pretty interesting – there was a tasting tour of the region's wineries, and a train journey through the highlands to bathe in a hot spring. And yet, my mother had plumped for the profoundly unremarkable Venus Line option. I guess it must have been the cheapest. It was still too early in the year for the yellow-orange daylilies for which the route was known.

And so in the end my mother, mastermind of the whole trip, stayed at home with my brother and Mariko, and my father and I were here, waiting to board the bus.

When I'd woken up that morning to find my father wasn't in the living room, my first thought was that maybe the whole thing had been called off, and for a moment the relief flooded through me.

'Did Dad decide not to go?' I asked my mother, who was sipping her morning coffee. My father, she informed me, had left the house at five, saying he wanted to 'breathe in the early morning Shinjuku air'.

After we'd been waiting under the ginkgoes for a while, someone in a blue safety vest appeared in front of a coach with a VENUS LINE sign and began calling people's names. We weren't anywhere near the first to be called, and I was just starting to think that maybe my mother had mistakenly cancelled the booking for all five of us, when I heard a shrill voice call out,

'Two in the name of Endo!'

The bus was practically full. Our seats were in the second row from the back, and walking the length of the bus to get to them, I felt people on either side of the aisle taking us in with curiosity. The only other mixed pairs on the tour were two sets of middle-aged people, clearly married couples. The rest were families with small children, and groups of women of various ages.

Watching my father's spindly frame moving down the aisle in front of me, I felt a sudden twinge of anxiety. They did realise that we were father and daughter, didn't they?

My father let me have the window seat. As we'd waited to board I'd been thinking to myself that once we were in our seats, we should find something to talk about. But now that we were sitting down, I realised it wasn't like there was a list of conversation topics provided for us in the mesh seat-pocket along with the map and the empty bag for our rubbish. For the time being, I decided to study the map of Nagano. My father just sat there, waiting for the bus to start moving.

I put a stick of gum in my mouth, and I was just about to offer one to my father when the tour guide began introducing herself and the engine started up.

It was good, my mother had said, to spend time alone with my father from time to time, and it was true – I realised I couldn't remember a single occasion when my father and I had gone somewhere just the two of us.

Quite possibly we had done when I was really young. But my father had never been what you'd call good with kids, and was by nature a person of few words and absolutely no jokes. When I reached a certain age, I made an effort to view him not as my father and rather as the man who was Takao Endo, but trying to see him from any other angle was like trying to bring two like poles of a magnet together – when I tried to get too close, Takao Endo would always go slithering away from me. Once, when my brother was in high school, he and my father had had a punch-up outside our front door. Seeing my father with his ashen face and delicate frame grappling my brawny, suntanned older brother was like watching a nursery-school kid taking on a professional sumo wrestler. I'd just got out of the bath and, rather than helping my mother who was doing her best to intervene, I stood there and felt any interest I'd previously had in my father evaporate along with the vapour rising from my skin. I was left with a feeling towards him that was neither quite pity nor scorn. I'd asked my brother what the fight had been about, but he wouldn't tell me. I knew my father must have had a good reason for letting things get to that point, but I'd already lost the interest it would have taken to ask him about it directly.

In the end, it must have been easiest for me to settle on the conclusion that my father was just my father, and nothing more. At that time I had plenty of other things to think about, so I gave up on the Takao Endo who always went skittering out of my reach, and forgot all about him.

Sitting there on the bus, I was doing my best to think of a time when my father and I had been out somewhere just the two of us. Maybe I was hoping to use it as a way of initiating conversation. The high-rise buildings had vanished from outside the windows, and we were now travelling down a road lined with trees that needed pruning and buildings with small windows set into their faded walls. Before I knew it, I'd drunk all the barley tea from the paper cup the guide had handed out, and as soon as the bus turned a corner, the empty cup toppled over and rolled across the tiny seatback table.

The tour guide had been telling us about the weather and the itinerary for the day in a soft, pleasant voice, but now she stopped, and the high-pitched voices of the female university students in the seats behind us took over. Sometimes at university, I sat around on the benches dotted around campus and chatted with the other girls from my class about nothing in particular. Now I wondered if at those times I sounded as young and empty-headed as the girls sitting behind me.

I tried shutting my eyes, but despite the early start I'd had, I didn't feel remotely sleepy. I fed another stick of gum into my mouth and took out my camera case from my tote bag. As of last month, I'd been going to a photography class a friend had invited me along to, and I'd bought the camera model the teacher there had recommended, for which I was paying in six instalments. It was a lot of money to splurge on a single item, for sure, but at least it would give me something to do with my time. That was a big part of the reason I'd originally agreed to come on this tour, too. I hadn't felt particularly enthusiastic about the prospect, but I'd accepted my mother's post-booking invitation on the grounds that it would, if nothing else, be a good opportunity to take some photos.

I hooked the strap around my neck and was playing around with the camera, peering into the viewfinder, when I caught my father looking at my hands. It was a look that might have signalled interest, but then again, might not have.

'Is that a single-lens reflex?'

'An SLR. Yeah.'

'You take photos now?'

'I'm going to classes.'

'When?'

'Every Thursday.'

'Oh, at university?'

'No, private ones.'

'Since when?'

'Last month.'

'Ah.'

The coach stopped at the lights. Outside the window was an old Japanese house with a sign that seemed disproportionally large for its flimsy, soot-darkened roof, white letters on a black background reading AOKI HARDWARE. Sensing the conversation with my father was probably over, I started thinking about what kind of things actually counted as 'hardware'. The first thing that came to mind was the wire mesh used for grilling *mochi*, the small sticky rice cakes eaten at New Year. Come to think of it, that had been the last time I'd been back to my parents' house – last New Year's.

'So, what will you photograph?'

Although he was asking me a question, my father's gaze was fixed on the cup of barley tea on the table in front of him and, just as when he issued commands to my mother like 'Fetch me a cloth, will you?', his tone lacked purpose. During the few seconds' pause that ensued, I was struck by the sense that we were performing some kind of a stand-up sketch called *Father and Daughter Have a Conversation.* And at the same time, I felt an odd pressure to keep on talking, maybe because of how much fun the girls behind us seemed to be having.

'The theme is fragments.'

'Fragments?'

'We've been told to take photos around the theme of fragments.'

'What do they mean by fragments?'

'Well, I don't really know, but I guess they mean things like that hardware sign over there, or that empty can under that tree, stuff like that.'

'Fragments, eh?'

'I imagine they're trying to get us to say that the world is full of fragments or whatever.'

'Right. Tricky stuff.'

The bus started to move again, and the AOKI HARDWARE sign disappeared from sight. With all its lumpy bits and sharp corners, the camera felt unwieldy in my hands. I found it hard to believe that there'd ever come a time when I'd get used to handling anything this heavy and irregularly shaped. The other students in the photography class who wore their cameras slung around their necks seemed to me almost ridiculously cool, but I sensed that I was somehow different to them. I put the camera in its case, then stashed it back inside my tote bag.

At the front of the bus, the tour guide stood up and started speaking into the mic, telling us that we'd soon be joining the motorway, and announcing how much time there was until the next service station stop.

At the service station, my father and I both needed the toilet, so we agreed to rendezvous in the shop. The toilets were the kind you only find in service stations, like miniature prisons. I stepped out from them and breathed the fresh air into my lungs. After all that time in the cool of the air-conditioned bus, it felt good to have the sun on my skin, and I decided to wait there for my father to emerge from the shop.

I perched myself on the lip of a flowerbed and was looking around me when I spotted my father also sat down beside a flowerbed, a little way away. He hadn't noticed me. There was no sign of him making his way into the shop either, despite our arranging to meet there. We still had a good ten minutes until the bus left, and I couldn't bring myself to stand up, so I stayed where I was and kept looking in his direction.

Just then, a white-haired old lady tripped up on the set of low steps leading up to the shop and fell in a way that looked dangerous even from that distance. My father jumped up immediately and helped her unsteadily to her feet. Then, together with the help of the other people who had gathered around the woman, he carried her into the gift shop. The speed at which my father had leapt into action had left me with a sense of slight shock. Feeling I'd witnessed something I shouldn't have, I dropped my eyes to my feet and examined the little clods of dirt lying around on the concrete. That was the first time I'd ever seen my father helping out a stranger like that. I suppose there must have been times when he'd helped me or my mother or my brother, but to recall them with anything like the same vividness as the scene I'd just witnessed would take time, and probably some kind of lead to go on.

The clock at the top of the ugly tower next to the shop showed it was almost time to go. I hoped that the old woman hadn't been badly injured, but by the time I started to move in the direction of the bus, my thoughts had taken a less virtuous turn, and I began wishing I'd had my camera with me so I could have got a shot of my father rescuing someone.

When the time came for the bus to set off, my father still wasn't back. He returned five minutes late, bowing his head to the people on both sides of the aisle in apology as he made his way towards me.

'Sorry for not waiting for you,' I said.

'Don't worry,' he said, and we fell into silence again.

Less than an hour later, we were at the cherry farm.

On the way there, the tour guide had told us a questionable story about the coal mines in one of the towns we had driven past. A long time ago, she said, when factories and coal mines had just started to be built in the town, there were a number of westerners living there, overseeing the running of it all. When the townspeople saw the westerners drinking red wine, which was still a rarity in Japan at the time, they took it for the blood of young girls who had come to work in the mines, and soon the whole town was in uproar.

'As if blood was ever that runny,' I said snidely as the guide was finishing up the anecdote, and my father said,

'Yeah.'

Pockets of laughter were still echoing around the bus. Feeling bored, I took out my camera again and got a few shots of the landscape outside the window.

My father didn't mention the thing with the old woman. Deciding there was no need for me to bring it up either, I said nothing.

We turned off the motorway and passed through a city area for a while. The mountains, which before had been no more than distant outlines, were now so close that you could make out all their crests and troughs, and the places dense with trees. The students, apparently tired of talking, had begun to doze off, but as soon as the cherry trees decked with little red fruits appeared outside the window, they woke up and began cooing excitedly, and the whole coach immediately filled with noise. As if thoroughly fed up of it all, the bus began to slow powerlessly to a halt. With my camera around my neck, I stepped out into the fresh air to find the women cheering and shrieking in ever-louder voices. It wasn't yet ten in the morning.

The cherry field was perched on top of a small hill. Sloping down and away from it was a buckwheat field, full of little white flowers that weren't quite in full bloom. Where the white patch ended was a row of dark green apple trees, beyond that a narrow road, then another spread of white flowers. The scene was so vast, it wouldn't fit in my field of vision. When I tried to take it all in, I lost my focus right away.

Even further in the distance lay the Japanese Alps, a cluster of huge blue rocks. I knew the Alps were divided into different sections, but whether these were the northern Alps or the central Alps or what, I had no idea. I was pretty sure my father wouldn't know either. Still, if there was a huge, sprawling mountain range somewhere called the Alps, I figured it probably wasn't too far-fetched to call whatever I could see in the distance its fragments. I pointed my camera towards it and took a few shots.

Passing through the net separating the farm path from the cherry fields, our tour group began picking the cherries of whatever tree took their fancy and tossing them into their mouths. The tree closest to me was large, and the branches easily in reach were already bare of cherries, but I managed to get a few by standing on my tiptoes. The cherries were a mixture of red, orange and yellow, and when I placed them on my palm under the sun, they didn't look like real food. I was thirsty, and my head felt kind of woozy in the way it did at the end of fifth period. Maybe sitting among all those people I didn't know had made me tense, without my really realising it. For a while I stood there, my head empty of thoughts, and simply popped cherries into my mouth, one after another.

When I started feeling a bit more myself, I went to look for my father. I found him surrounded by a group of middle-aged women, beside a tree of sweet red cherries. I wondered if they'd mistaken him for a farm employee. He was plucking the dark-red fruits growing on the higher branches and those tucked away inside tangles of twigs, and handing them, one by one, to the women.

My father's face was the unobtrusive type, and he was by temperament an undemanding man. He seemed largely indifferent to getting ahead in the world, but nor did he go out drinking and frittering his money away or anything like that. Apart from his height, there was really nothing about him that registered as masculine.

I tried to imagine my father thirty years younger, around the same age as I was. Would I find him attractive? In less than the time than it took me to eat a cherry, I'd reached my conclusion: no way. If anything, I tended to go for men who were the exact opposite of my father – talkative types, who were always sunny and cheerful. The guy I was seeing at the moment was so unfailingly optimistic that it sometimes took me aback. When I'd told him that we were going on a family outing to pick cherries, he'd been positively envious: 'Wow, your family's so close! Maybe I should take mine on a tour or something, too.'

Achieving such clarity on the matter, though, made me feel suddenly sorry for my father, so I loaded my palm up with cherries and went up behind him.

'Could you get that one behind that leaf, please?' one of the women was saying.

'Which one?'

'To the right. Stretch your arm... further... Yes, that's it!'

No sooner had he dropped a glossy red fruit onto the palm of one woman, the next woman would approach with her request. It seemed like there was no time for my father to be eating any cherries himself. But that didn't appear to bother him in the slightest, and he kept doing exactly as the women instructed. As his daughter, it didn't make for a particularly pleasant scene to be observing, but just as with the old woman back in the service station, the sight of my father helping people out as a fully functional man was like watching a household pet suddenly starting to speak in human language. My curiosity won out, and I couldn't peel my eyes away.

Noticing me behind him, my father pointed at the slender Bing cherry tree, which had been plundered of virtually all its fruits, and said,

'You want one?'

'There aren't any left on that one.'

Now another woman, whose keen eyes had spotted a remaining cherry nestling behind a leaf on a high branch, tugged at my father's polo shirt. Before I'd finished all the cherries on my palm, my father was being escorted away by the group of women to another tree.

We ate our lunch in the Cherry Shack, an old wooden house that had been converted into a visitors' centre, complete with gift shop and restaurant. The miso soup they served, which was loaded up with profuse quantities of some mysterious type of mushroom, went down very well with my father, who remarked with every sip,

'Mm, this is good.'

'Mum makes soup like this, though.'

'Does she?'

'Just with fewer mushrooms.'

'Yes, probably.'

'There's just no need for this many mushrooms. We're not forest bears here.'

My father let out a sigh and took a little sip from his cup of barley tea. I thought again about him helping the old woman in the service station. For some reason, that scene was refusing to merge into the folds of my memory, lingering stubbornly in the corner of my mind. It brought up the same kinds of feelings as when I'd seen my father fighting my brother those years ago – feelings that were already making their way downhill towards the conclusion that I shouldn't have come today after all.

'Blimey, this is good though.'

'It's full of weird mushrooms!'

'Mushrooms are weird things to begin with.'

'What? Shimeji and shiitake aren't weird. They're just normal vegetables.'

'What do you mean by "normal"?'

'I mean they're just what people normally eat.'

My father sipped his soup again without replying. It seemed possible that my words had passed straight through him and out the other side, because the unmade-up woman sitting beside him was now showing an abnormal interest in me.

Something about the way she was staring so intently and the way my father had fallen silent made me feel that, even though here I was, 20 years old and a full-grown adult, I still wasn't mature enough to have a proper discussion with my father about mushrooms or the relative worth of things. The feeling was as tangible as the tables, the food and the women I could see around me, and the plastic chopsticks, the chair and the T-shirt that my body was touching.

'I'm going for a walk,' I said, and left the restaurant.

Outside the Cherry Shack, wooden houses and apple fields stretched off into the distance, until they were interrupted a good way off by a road. I set off down a path dividing up the fields. In the distance were the same kinds of Alps as I'd seen from the cherry field. I took out my phone, thinking I'd send a photo to my boyfriend who, somewhere way beyond those distant mountains in far-off Tokyo, would doubtless be either playing mah-jong or taking a nap, but it was out of range. I put the phone away again, and was standing there with my hands on my hips staring out at the fields when it came to me that it wasn't just phone signal I wasn't picking up. Being here, I felt like I was out of range of any possible kind of enjoyment. I took a few photographs, and started walking again.

What did the people living around here find to enjoy in their lives? Probably things like picking apples and looking for fireflies and riding their bikes around. Even steeped in a landscape this quiet and soothing, did people still hole themselves up at home on the internet all day?

Dawdling along thinking about these things, I looked up and was surprised to see my father, 100 metres or even further in the distance. Strange as it was, my instinctive reaction to seeing a member of my family that far away was to wave to him and alert him to my presence – even though if he'd been any closer, I'd probably have done my best to make sure he didn't see me.

'Dad!' I called out, waving. Arms folded behind his back, gazing at something, my father looked towards me and lifted his hand. Then he raised his arm to consult his watch and began to make his way slowly towards me. I stopped where I was and waited for him, pawing at the soil with the toe of my shoe. As my father came nearer, I could see he was saying something.

'Hm?'

'We've got to go.'

'Already?'

'The bus is going to leave. Aren't you wearing a watch?'

'No, I don't have one.'

'The guide said to be back by two.'

'Oh.'

My father turned his back to me and started walking off.

'How did you get that far, when I left before you?'

'I came out the back entrance.'

'What were you doing?'

'There was a house over there with a nice garden. I was just looking at it.'

'What kind of a garden?'

'It had a big arch of roses and the walls were sky blue. Flowers in the garden.'

'What? An arch of roses and sky-blue walls? That sounds amazing. Are you serious?'

'Yeah.'

'Where was it?'

'Over there.' My father turned around and pointed back at the path from which he'd come.

'If that's true, I'm going to go take a photo.'

'We've only got five minutes. We better get back.'

'It'll only take a second. If I run I'll just about make it. We've come all this way.'

'Okay, then run. I'll go ahead and tell the guide.'

'Okay. Thanks.'

I broke into a run down the path between the fields. Once I'd started, I felt like I could go faster, so I started running properly like we'd been taught to do in PE lessons, lifting my arms and tilting my upper body forward. The camera bumped painfully against my stomach, so I held it steady with one hand as I ran. When I stopped beside a little red well and turned around, my father was nowhere to be seen.

Figuring that this must have been close to where my father had been standing before, I looked around in every direction, but I couldn't see the house he was talking about. I tried standing on my tiptoes and craning my neck, crouching down, going a little way into the field beside me, checking everything I thought could be my blind spots, but whatever I did, there was no sign of any house with sky-blue walls.

'It's not here,' I said out loud to myself, and felt the irritation suddenly surge up inside me. I wanted to rip out my sides, aching from the running, and hurl them in anger at the tranquil scene stretched out in front of me.

Instead I held onto them with one hand, gripped my camera with the other, and set off at a jog toward the restaurant down the path I'd come from.

This time it was me who had to travel down the aisle of the bus bowing my head in apology to the people on either side. My father stood up to let me in to the window seat.

'It wasn't there.'

'What?'

'There was no sky-blue house.'

'There was.'

'There was not. I looked in every possible direction.'

'Are you sure you didn't go the wrong way?'

'Did you actually even see it, Dad?'

'I saw it.'

Whether I'd not run far enough, or my father had pointed in the wrong direction – the thought of either possibility just made me feel angry all over again.

'You never know with you,' I said and slumped against the window. And yet my eyes were still kind of searching for the house my father said he'd seen, the garden with the rose arch. The bus slid past a few apple fields and people's houses, and by the time we got onto the wide two-lane roads, I'd stopped caring.

The tour guide was talking about the origin of the Venus Line route, to which we were now headed. I took out my mobile and wrote my boyfriend a text:

What you up to? The cherry-picking tour is LONG.

I was picking up signal again now.

'Kiriko,' a voice woke me. 'We're here.'

I opened my eyes and saw we were in the car park for the Mount Kirigamine rest stop. I'd slept through the whole of the Venus Line, totally missing the red azaleas that were in season at the moment. As the bus parked up slowly, the tour guide was advising people, off the mic, to be sure to try the free samples of quince juice in the gift shop.

The crisp, cool air outside the bus felt nice. With nothing better to do, I decided to head up the hill across the road, a 20-minute round trip. Uninvited, my father tagged along beside me.

'Apparently you can try quince juice in the shop.'

'Yeah, so she was saying.'

'We can have some after.'

'If we have time.'

'How do you usually measure time without a watch?'

'Why would I need to *measure* time?'

'Aren't you late for lectures and stuff?'

'I've got a clock on my phone.'

'It's very convenient to have the time on your wrist, you know.'

'Mobiles are convenient too, Dad.'

I looked around and saw a white hang-glider pressing in on us directly over-head, looking like it was making to land on the other side of the hill. My father tipped his head back and walked along like that in silence.

On the top of the hill was a bell mounted to the top of a concrete arch, the kind they often had in wedding chapels in hotels, with a sign beside it that read The Bell of Happiness. A pair of twin boys, wearing an identical outfit in differ-ent colours, were tugging the bell rope over and over with wild energy. On the other side of the platform on which the bell-arch was mounted was an empty chairlift leading down to the bottom of the slope. I guessed this place must be used as a ski slope in winter. The hang-glider from before had landed some way beyond the bottom of the slope.

This virtually motionless scene slowly soaked up the incessant ringing of the Bell of Happiness like a thick paper napkin.

I sat down on a bench positioned directly in front of the bell-arch and watched the two boys absorbed in their frenetic ringing. The more I looked, the more I had the strange sense that I knew all of this: the mottled pattern of the arch's peeling white paint, the fraying rope, this crisp air, the wide-open sky and fields, all of it. I rifled back through my hazy memories of summer, and this place – which is to say, the three elements of the bell, the distant mountains, and the cool air – came back to me, still indistinct but crystallised now into the form of a single photo.

Leaving enough space for a small child to fit between us, my father sat down on the bench beside me.

'Dad, I just had a thought. Have we been here before?'

'What?'

'I have this feeling like I came here before, with you, and Mum, and Eiji. When I was in primary school, or younger even.'

'Yeah, we have. I thought you'd forgotten.'

'Wait, did you know that all along?'

'No, I only just remembered myself.'

I began to work very carefully at recovering the memory, which seemed like it could go flying off with even the tiniest of movements.

I was pretty sure I'd seen the photograph when I'd been looking through old family albums at New Year, a few years back. I was on the far left, sitting on the base of the arch with a terrycloth blanket draped over my head, looking pale and grumpy. Lined up next to me were my mother, my brother and my father, all standing. Interposed between the four of us and the overcast sky behind was the very bell I was looking at now. Back then, the only worlds I'd known were my house and my nursery school, but still, there I was, sitting in the spot where the boys were running around now, dangling my sandalled feet towards the camera.

'I think we took a photo with the bell.'

'Really? Where?'

'We took a photo of all four of us, in front of that bell over there. It's in the album.'

'Oh, that bell over there. Right.'

Even knowing this, I felt no desire to take a photo of me and my father in front of the bell arch, or anything so sentimental.

The idea that now, more than a decade later, the little kids in that photograph knew their fair share about the world and led their own lives – in my brother's case, even had a family of his own – sounded like something someone had made up. But then again, here I was now with my father, actually looking at that bell, and my brother was at home caring for his baby daughter, so another part of me felt like it must be the photograph that was the made-up bit.

What would my mother be doing now? Was my brother taking proper care of Mariko? Or was he just lolling around reading? As if thinking the same thoughts as me, my father mumbled, out of the blue,

'I wonder what Mum and Eiji are up to.'

'Not much, probably. I wonder if Mariko's temperature's gone down.'

'Who knows.'

'Eiji really should have come with us. There was no need for him to stay at home, not with Mum there.'

'I imagine he's tired.'

'I'm tired too, though.'

'Hmm.'

'What about you? You're tired too, no?'

'No.'

'You're not tired?'

'Not as much as you.'

'Do I really seem that tired?'

'You just said you were tired.'

I left a little meaningful pause, then said forcefully,

'You know, there really is no point having a conversation with you, Dad.'

My father gave a dry little laugh. 'Ha. Ha.'

'It's like dropping stones into water or something.'

'You think?'

'You were a fully grown adult last time we came here. Surely you must have remembered?'

'It honestly only just came back to me. It was a long time ago.'

'Didn't Mum say anything about it?'

'I imagine she's probably forgotten too.'

I propped my arms up on my knees and dropped my head into my hands, mussing up my hair. Through the gaps in my hair, the cool breeze skimmed my scalp.

'At this rate, you're going to forget everything.'

'Yeah, probably,' my father said with a weak laugh that was soon drowned out by the chime of the bell.

'More to the point, if you don't assert yourself in some way, then we're all going to forget about you.'

'That's okay. It's like I'm not really here, anyway.'

'What do you mean by that?'

This time I fell silent, without meaning to.

I thought about my father, back when I was living with him. My father, who blended in so perfectly with the various tableaux of our house – the post-dinner table littered with empty plates, the balcony chair with its torn cushion, the storage space under the stairs – that he became a part of them. Stepping out of the house at eight on the dot in one of his grey suits – who knew how many he actually owned – he would instantly be lost among the convoy of people making their way to the station.

Even now, I couldn't see my father clearly in the way I'd seen the crisp, well-defined outlines of those Alps, whichever section they might have been.

'It's just fragments,' my father said, unexpectedly.

'What did you just say?'

'It's all fragments.'

'What do you mean by *all*?'

'What we're seeing now. Everything that's here. Me, you, that bell, all of it. There, that's my assertion.'

I'd been conceptualising fragments as stuff like the AOKI HARDWARE sign, and the empty can on the road, and the slivers of mountain. But if it was as my father said, and everything we were seeing now, everything here was a fragment of something else, then what shape did that other thing take, and how big was it?

'Right,' I said. I stood up, setting out back for the bus.

From behind me, I heard my father say, 'Don't you want to take any photos?'

On the way back, there were bad traffic jams on the motorway, and the only way of alleviating the boredom was to sleep. But although I shut my eyes and leaned my head against the window frame, I couldn't fall asleep properly like I had during the Venus Line. Until not long ago, the university girls behind me had been moaning like anything about the traffic, but now they were out like lights. My father had dropped off way before them. His pale hands, relatively full in comparison to his meagre frame, lay half upturned on his knees, draped across the creased fabric of his shorts.

As we drew close to Shinjuku station, my father woke of his own accord. Then it was my turn to close my eyes and pretend to be asleep.

'Blimey, it was hot today,' I heard him mumble to himself. I almost found myself answering, 'Yeah, it was.'

Back in the house, Mariko was still in bed, my mother was busy preparing dinner and my brother was sitting on the sofa in the living room reading a computer magazine. I handed him the box of Ptarmigan Town cream-filled wafers we'd bought at the service station on the way home. He thanked me and began munching them as he read.

'How's Mariko?'

'Well, her temperature's gone down, but she still seems a bit under the weather.'

'Is it okay for you to be just sitting reading like that?'

'It's not like she's going get better faster if I'm sat there by her side staring at her the whole time.'

'I reckon Mum's gonna tell Rikako, you know.'

'Man, you're such a child! Are you that bitter that I didn't come?'

'It's hard being alone with Dad. Really hard.'

My brother lifted his face from his book and peered at me as if studying a rare insect species. Five or six of the wafer-wrapper ptarmigans lay scattered across the patchwork throw.

'You find him hard? He's like the easiest person ever.'

'There's nothing there! No backbone, no drive, nothing.'

'Were you hoping there would be?'

My father came into the room, having changed into the clothes he wore inside the house. He moved past us with his papery footsteps and went through into the kitchen.

'No,' I said, and my brother immediately lost interest and returned to his magazine. Then my mother called us to come and help with dinner.

In the end, it took more than three weeks for me to develop the photos from that day. The week after the tour, the rainy season hit and, feeling loath to venture out of the house any more than strictly necessary, I left my camera in its case on top of the TV stand. For the photography class, I selected a few photos that I'd taken previously, and submitted them for the assignment. The photo studio was entering our efforts into a contest in a magazine, with the results to be announced in two months' time, but I'd abandoned any hopes of winning from the get-go.

Finally, with the rainy season looking set to end, I made it to pick up the photos one evening after work. It had been raining until early afternoon, and as I cycled to the electrical store where I'd put them in for developing, I could feel through the soles of my feet on the pedals that the asphalt was softer than usual. Now and then, the white lines on the road flashed as if lit up.

I came out of the shop and stood beside the vending machine in the car park so I could leaf through the photos, but all of them were taken from a similar sort of angle, and there was nothing about them that stood out. They were all the mediocre kind of snaps that would suit harmless titles like *Nature* or *The Beauty of Japan*.

Trying to find at least something to like about them, I leaned against the side of the vending machine and went through the photos again, this time examining each one carefully. There were blurry shots taken inside the bus, shots of the buckwheat fields, the mountains in the distance, people eating cherries, the path between the rice fields, Mount Kirigamine from the hill – they were just cut-outs from scenes, all of them, without the sounds or smells that had once accompanied them.

On the third go through, as fatigue and hopelessness were starting to kick in, I made a discovery. There, in one of the shots of the cherry trees taken from the buckwheat field was my father's profile, surrounded by all the middle-aged women. I'd had no idea when I'd taken it that he was in the shot.

He was standing beneath a tree over by the back right-hand corner of the field, surrounded by the crowd of women eager for cherries, yet oddly enough, he didn't seem to be looking at any of them. His face was slightly lifted, his mouth was half-open, and his expression was impossible to read, but his profile was definitely, unmistakably my father's.

His gaze – looking at nothing, saying nothing in particular, just staring out into space – cut through the photograph at an angle.

As I stared at his profile, it came to me that I had known my father properly all along, and, at the same time, that this person in the photo was a complete stranger to me.

Through my shoulder, I could feel the heat and the tiny vibrations coming off the vending machine. Sensing somehow that they were going to disrupt the scene in the photo, guarded over as it was by endless silence, I stood up straight, away from the machine. My father's gaze passed out of the side of the photo and headed towards a pale-coloured star, which hung between the clouds in the eastern sky.

A. K. BLAKEMORE

POETRY

MAY

you slid into my life as though
a witch's smock — a sun poem.

fat bee on a bright brick wall
atrocious swan of love

we roll apart
our grave-beds loose and hot

*

i have so many bouquets
it's like somebitch died —

using love
as a bulwark
against modernity's axiomatic selfishness
which i realise may after all be my great theme like
fuck

TINY VIOLETFLAVOURED

here i am of sunday
and earth
rotoxid — fortunate
for all i am not very giving of myself

the mad winds in trees behind the houses and
indulgent baby

bad
but better than Lars von Trier

like depression
all your friends have had me

affirmation: even the slug (who is most profane)
trails a platinum appliqué
of artistic tragedy

MY MARRIAGE THROAT

and what really mattered
were the cancers we metastasised along the way —

a shame of spotted blood on the guest-pillow.
the other afternoon i almost whistled after the hatchet-faced man on his red bicycle
like
pursue me!

desire very icicles
cracking fantastically from a wingmirror -

sorrow, o no
too many times left dry.

my marriage throat —
behind the suburb's water-coloured fascia
a window filled with orchids in the fluted bonnets
of benighted spiritualists

what would it mean to shrink myself? pirate mini golf
and evenings spent choked to supernatancy
by well-beloved hand.

MERNET LARSEN   INTERVIEW

Enter the world of Mernet Larsen, and you will find yourself on unstable ground. Tables and chairs pitch too steeply to support their contents, teacups and notepads stretch impossibly away from your fingertips, passersby elongate like rubber bands.

Look closer, and the skin of a Mernet Larsen painting reveals its bones: pencil sketches are sometimes visible, and tracing paper leaves raised edges behind certain sections the artist has collaged. Although often misunderstood as a product of early computer graphics, Larsen's paintings employ a distinctive style of geometric figuration informed by a wide range of cultural references, from Piero della Francesca and Kazimir Malevich to traditional Japanese scrolls. Larsen, who is 78, has been making paintings on canvas for more than five decades, but in 2000 came to a profound turning point in her career. She began to work from abstract paintings that caught her eye and translate them into recognisable figures and situations: planes of colour became human faces, buildings, or baby's bassinets. Larsen began toying with perspective, too – as if stoned on Alice's mushroom cap, everything in her paintings became topsy-turvy. Spaces of intense vertigo, these paintings depict a world in which established hierarchies have been upended and nothing is ever fully certain.

Although Larsen has exhibited extensively throughout her career, she did not receive widespread critical attention until a 2012 solo exhibition at Johannes Vogt Gallery, New York, followed by a show at Various Small Fires in LA. Her work has since been collected by museums such as the Whitney Museum of American Art, New York and the Carnegie Museum of Art, Pittsburgh. This conversation took place in June at James Cohan Gallery, New York, as Larsen's recent solo exhibition, *Situation Rooms* (2018), was set to close there. Larsen is Professor Emeritus at the University of South Florida, Tampa, where she taught for nearly forty years, and in several paintings of 'faculty meetings' attendant teachers with wan expressions sit around grey folding tables on stippled linoleum floors. A trick of reverse perspective renders distant figures much larger than those in the foreground. Other paintings depict more serious 'situation rooms', where inattentiveness could be critical: for example US Cabinet meetings, some characters recognisable by their hair or skin tones, such as Hillary Clinton and Barack Obama. These seem to highlight the farcical pageantry of diplomatic negotiation: rows of hands clasped in practised patterns. Though their subjects can be serious, Larsen's paintings are deliriously funny.   EVAN MOFFITT

TWR   You have a distinct and immediately recognisable style, and have had for some decades, but your paintings also seem to reference a wide variety of sources. Other critics have cited 1980s computer graphics like *Minecraft*, the design from that period like Memphis, and then historical precedents like Synthetic Cubism, Russian Constructivism. How did you first arrive at your geometric style?

ML   My reasoning goes back a long way, and it's sort of circular. I've been making the geometric work you're referring to since around 2000, but there were many phases leading up to that. I began in the 1960s working very figuratively, and I thought of myself as a narrative painter. When I started school in the late 1950s, it was the heyday of Abstract Expressionism, when figures were absent. I was studying at the University of Florida, and I was actually going to drop out of the art department and study philosophy or music instead, because people like Josef Albers or Willem de Kooning just didn't speak to the particulars of my life. But I had a really great teacher called Hiram D. Williams; probably nobody's heard of him by now but at one time MoMA was filled with his paintings. And Williams said to me: just go out and do it – go out and draw what you see. It was a revelation.

TWR   *Last Tango* (1975) depicts a kind of ballroom scene, with couples dancing and dining. The room is detailed enough that we can make out the grain of the wood panelling on the walls. How did you transition away from this figurative, photographic mode?

ML   In the mid 70s, I lived in New York for a few years. I was mostly sitting around looking at people in Washington Square or the Met cafeteria, and paintings like *Last Tango* reflected this. Eventually, I felt I'd become too much of a spectator. I wanted to paint solidity, weight and volume, but I'd become reliant on photographic information – on surface. So I started studying Renaissance techniques. There are 'How To' books on Vermeer or Rembrandt, with step-by-step instructions: where to begin, what kind of paint brush to use, and so on... I actually got a couple of paintings to superficially look like Vermeer. I was particularly looking at the work of the fifteenth-century Italians, and one of their techniques was to begin drawing figures as geometric solids. I was doing sketches and then laying out

all the tones and details, but I found that I liked my pictures better when the figures were just geometric solids. So this, to answer your original question, is where the geometric figures began. These paintings from the early 80s are precursors to the ones I make now – but there was a period of abstraction between.

TWR   During that period of abstraction, the figure seemed to disappear almost entirely. I'm thinking here of *Sadhu Arching* (1996), for example, or *Golfer* (1997) in which the presence of figures only becomes apparent upon reading the titles. Did you have these subjects in mind when you began those paintings?

ML   I was trying to find a new syntax. From the mid-80s to 1999, I was working very improvisationally, very involved with process and physical surface: scraping, burying, collaging, peeling, adding sheet rock compound to the paint, so the paintings were kind of like old walls. I had no subject matter in mind, but as I worked, subject matter would emerge. Michelangelo once said there was a figure embedded in every piece of marble and his job was to chip it out. I felt something similar in *Golfer*: that there was a character embedded in my paintings, and it was up to me to discover what it was.

Disillusioned with both photography and conventional figure painting, I had also begun to look at abstract and non-western paintings as possible springboards for a different kind of space. In 1985, I deconstructed El Lissitzky's *Proun 12E* (1923), for example, to see and decipher it in as many ways as I could, as if it really was a representational painting. I began to see Lissitzky's composition as a floor plan. Then I would flip it around, looking for a face or a narrative. Each reading that I superimposed onto it would make me sensitive to another painting possibility. I began to see the Lissitzky as an image of shoppers carrying parcels, although the other readings still haunted it, so it was ambiguous, abstract. I playfully titled it *Shoppers* (2001), while not insisting viewers read it that way. Over time, my improvisational method became very minimal, reductive, and, in the end, I became frustrated. I began to feel I was denying myself depth, colour, volume – and stories, the things I loved about Renaissance painting. I wondered what would happen if I tried to make a Renaissance-like painting that took into consideration some of the things I had learned over the last fifteen

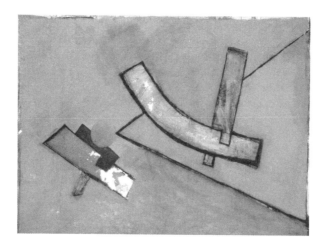

years (and that the art world had learned over the last few centuries). It's impossible to go back to the conventional realism of that era – that way is barred by the angel with the flaming sword – because we know too much about perception, too much about physics, too much about the world.

TWR   Did you want to make a painting that was more transparently constructed, in the way that Renaissance paintings were?

ML   I wanted to move out of abstraction, but Western realism has been picked apart across the last century and understood to be a total construct. So if I was going to use some of realism's conventions, I felt they had to be visible as conventions. They couldn't look like illusion; they had to be visible as toys – something you play with to make space. I decided to play with other conventions too, like parallel perspective, where you have parallel lines that never converge, and to use these conventions in the way that architects use them. I had already based some of my abstract compositions on Japanese narrative painting from the twelfth century, that also uses parallel perspective. I love the kind of space that never converges but still feels like it has depth. This is how I moved into the period that I'm in now – tapping back into the Renaissance drawing strategies that I'd been exploring in the 80s.

TWR   So the bones were there all along?

ML   It was a dialectical process of going in this direction, and then going to the opposite extreme, and then synthesising the two things. Twenty years after I'd made the first version of *Shoppers*, I decided to literalise it, to make it readable. Rather than saying to everybody, 'Oh, you can see it as this if you want to, or you can see that if you want to', I decided to commit – to show it a certain way. So that led to *Shoppers* (2001) in which you can clearly see two people carrying their packages.

It's an old ploy really, to Rorschach things onto other things. Leonardo da Vinci would bunch up sheets and study the wrinkles and get ideas for his work – I just read a biography of him. Some Surrealists did it too. I'm prone to Rorschaching paintings and other things. As in Rorschach's famous inkblot test [where subjects' perceptions of the abstract shapes of inkblots are recorded and analysed for insight into personality], I think the process draws out of me interests and priorities I didn't know I had. I've been doing it all my adult life. I'll take a Japanese narrative painting and turn it upside down and try to see another story in it. At first, I have to do a lot of work to 'unsee' the original, so that I stop seeing a building on its head. But eventually, the new thing emerges.

TWR   You start with a structure, often a representational image, and try to see another image within it. Do you think of this as moving from the concrete to the abstract and back again?

ML   When I think of Malevich or Picasso or any of the early modernist painters, they often seem to move from a conventional view of realism to abstracting it. I'm moving in the other direction.

Malevich had an interesting journey. He did all these wonderful, vertiginous paintings during his constructivist period and then returned to painting figures in his later life – peasants and so on. His figures are infused with geometry, but they are also very conventional paintings, spatially. His use of the horizon, for instance – horizons are my enemy.

TWR   Why?
ML   Horizons establish the ground plane; as long as the horizon is visible or implicit, you are oriented. I want the viewer to be *disorientated*, to not know exactly where they are relative to what they're seeing. There is a related disorientation in Indian, Persian, medieval and Japanese painting, and some early modernism. Instead of being a spectator, as in a photograph, you are both inside and outside, 'wearing' the situation, I like to think.

TWR   As you talk about revealing the conventions of perspective, I think of the radicalism of Cézanne. In his paintings, perspective is skewed and things are imbalanced. They don't aspire to the orderliness of a Renaissance painting. They're very messy.
ML   Cézanne is probably the most important painter to me; he took the world apart and put it back together again in another way, as opposed to reducing it or expressing it or exaggerating it. Have you ever come across Erle Loran's book *Cézanne's Compositions* (1943)? I don't know if you can even find it anymore, it's in such bad repute

– and undeservedly so. Loran went to southern France in the 1950s and he found the exact place where Cézanne would have been standing while painting Mont Sainte-Victoire, and he took photographs. Loran then analyses what Cézanne did, drawing arrows to show the shifts and movements of the planes. I mean it's crazy and wacky. But Cézanne's aspiration and achievement was to make his paintings solid and durable (not messy): 'like the art of the old masters', he said, but taking into account perception in time.

TWR   With many of your paintings, such as *Dawn* and *Dusk* (both 2012) there's a sense of instability or vertigo.
ML   Yes, I want the viewer to feel disorientated – that's what vertigo is, a not being able to find where you are relative to what's around you. *Dawn* and *Dusk* are based on a composition by El Lissitzky. I often use his paintings as springboard/Rorschachs, because they project disorientation. That sense of vertigo is a lot more pronounced in others, especially in those where I started using reverse perspective. *Landscape with a Dirt Road (from Poussin)* (2011), for example, is a reverse perspective rendering of a Poussin painting.

TWR   You use yourself as the vanishing point in your faculty paintings, and the effect is psychologically disorientating. For example in *Explanation* (2007), in which the figures that are further away almost loom over you as the viewer.

ML   Perversely, I always wanted to paint a faculty meeting, because that's where I've spent a lot of my life. But every time I tried to do a faculty painting, they were pretty boring to look at. And so I began to try using parallel perspective, and then one day I had the idea of bringing in a vanishing point. I thought: what if I, as the painter, became the vanishing point? What if I was infinitely small? This is how the whole situation grew. It means that the further away people around the table were, the bigger they would be. The wonderful thing was that this way of working gave me a way to make those images feel fresh, worth looking at.

TWR   How did you go about constructing these compositions?

ML   I took some photos of a faculty meeting, traced the tables, then turned the traced tables upside down. That was the starting point. Then I started to measure the people, tried to draw them accurately in reverse perspective. But the problem was, they all began to look like Lego people – too blocky, and I couldn't stand them. I had to completely rethink and redraw their proportions and sizes, while retaining the 'accurate' reverse perspective tables. I didn't want the images to seem as if they had been made using a system or computer. Of course, many viewers see them as being done by a system, but if you look carefully you can see that there's nothing systematic or consistent about them, and that the figures have impossible proportions.

TWR   Are you interested in making your process visible to viewers? There are often pencil marks discernible on the surface of your paintings, which seem like useful cues to that process.

ML   If I'm working from a photograph, as in the faculty meetings and situation rooms, I try to keep the colours of the furniture and clothing and skin, the same relationships that were in the photographs. In other words, I try not to change anything, except for the structure of the image (which is a drastic change). If I'm working from, say, an El Lissitzky painting, I try to remain absolutely true to his structure, but develop a legible subject matter – in a way, the reverse of when I work from photos I take.

I start with a very small thumbnail sketch, enlarge it very precisely to a 19 x 24 piece of paper, where I decide on basic colour. I then copy it very precisely to a large canvas. When you're working geometrically, there's a tendency to straighten everything out, or regularise, as you change the scale. I wanted to retain the spirit of whatever it was that I liked to begin with. Once it's painted in on the large canvas, the painting really begins! I may spend two or three months working out details and surface, often painting possible details on tracing paper, wetting the paper and trying things out, like trying on clothes. When I get a hand, for example, right, I paste it on. I do a lot of drawing at this stage too. So the collaging and much drawing remains visible, which I like. I hate the surface of acrylic, so the tracing paper and various gels transform that.

TWR   The body of work on show at James Cohan Gallery includes scenes of political summits. We've been seeing lots of images of theatrical summits between world leaders in recent news, and a couple of your figures appear recognisable.
ML   Yes, some actual people are in there, though minuscule! I started looking at pictures of the White House, the Cabinet Room and the Situation Room. My husband [the artist Roger Clay Palmer] deals with political subject matter in his work, so the TV news is ubiquitous in our lives. I became fascinated by those images. I wanted to do something with this environment – the rose-red floors with gold stars and the really incredibly oval table in the Cabinet Room, and the beige walls, blue carpet and the TV screens in the Situation Room.

TWR   In faculty meetings, as in corporate boardrooms, there are typically certain large personalities and other people who can't get a word in. Do you think about those kinds of social dynamics?
ML   I do not – but I accept people reading them into my paintings. Working from photographs, I dealt with the Cabinet Room and the Situation Room in the same way that I dealt with the faculty photographs. Again, I tried to stay as true to the photographs as I could. The photographs I had were tiny things from Google, and there are fifty people in the frame, and so all you can really take from them are the poses, the gestures, the clothing. In *Cabinet Meeting (with Coffee)* (2018), I used

reverse perspective, so there's a woman with a coffee at the far end of the table, and then everyone around her is reduced to tiny characters. It's the Obama administration, and you can identify Obama in a couple of my paintings, probably because of the colour of his skin, Clinton because of her hair – even though they're tiny, and totally insignificant in the structure of the painting.

TWR   Is Obama's size the result of the formal rules that you set for yourself, rather than a political comment?
ML   Definitely not a political comment, at least not consciously! One thing I've learned is that people notice size, because size implies and infers hierarchy. The first thing that people seem to notice – especially people who don't have a background in art – is that some people in the image are big and some people are small. They notice this before they notice that the perspective has been reversed. My brother-in-law had this great revelation after he saw one of my paintings. He'd never looked at art in his life, and was driving down the highway in his car and he looked down at his hand and he thought, 'My hand is big and that other car down there is little.' It was an epiphany about normal perspective because most people do not perceive normal perspective as size differences.

TWR   That may be why it says on the rearview mirror of certain vehicles, 'objects in this mirror are larger than they appear'.

ML   People often don't see perspective, so they don't see my paintings as a reversal of perspective; what they see is size. *Explanation* (2007) often engenders a dialogue about race and gender. In the painting, the two largest figures are a black man and a white woman – the only ones on the faculty, perhaps. So, in a way, it's poetic justice. You could say they've become the main characters. But if you saw the photograph that this is based on, where the same two figures are small and far away and the white guys are closer to my camera and therefore bigger, you'd probably notice those two people the least.

TWR   There's a sort of humorous touch to your painting, a kind of wry detachment. Do you feel that this is necessary to make people notice things that they might not otherwise? For example, in the case of your brother-in-law, by manipulating his vision as viewer, you helped him to see things the way they really were.
ML   I want all my paintings to result in people seeing. Who was it that said artists make people see what they are blind to? I'm in the middle of reading Rachel Cusk's novel *Kudos* (2018). I've decided she's my favourite writer right now. She creates these impossible situations in her writing, but you sort of accept them. She is straight-faced in her delivery, so you're never aware that she's trying to make you laugh – but it's funny. The humour sort of sneaks up on you. And she can be very cutting towards people that she's dealing with, but she's never judgmental, she always sees

them in their full humanity. Even the people she makes terrible fun of, she rescues their humanity out of it. That seems like a worthy goal.

In a similar way to Cusk, who is always dealing with her own character in her writing, I'm thinking through myself when I'm dealing with political situations. I'm imagining these people around the table as having lives, getting up for breakfast, or sitting around at home. I want to put humanity into these situations, because that's often what is missing. You know, I'm often asked if I'm trying to depict the repression of feeling, the way that in the boardroom people are not allowed to show emotions, even as they discuss earth-shaping issues. But that's not right at all. I'm not trying to do people who are like automatons or robots.

TWR   I find their facial expressions revealing. There's a lot of variety. You're in this fishbowl environment where you're able to observe the slightest difference in someone's composure. Some of the faces seem very bemused or bored. In *Cabinet Meeting (with Coffee)* or *Cup Tricks* (2018), for instance, delightful, minute differences convey a lot of personality.
ML   The facial expressions are actually sort of random. I don't want them to look like puppets, but at the same time, I want them to be very reserved, not letting you quite know what they're thinking. I want them to be like Cusk somehow, like her central character [Faye, the narrator in Cusk's trilogy of novels *Outline* (2014), *Transit* (2016) and *Kudos* (2018)], who is interested and

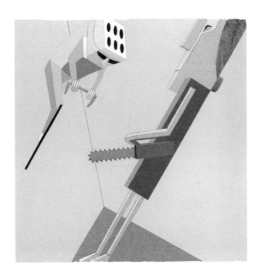

observant but who never shows her cards. She's somewhere near all the people she describes, but you never quite see where she stands in all this.

TWR   Cusk is very perceptive of people's fundamental awkwardness and anxiety, the qualities that come through in our facial expressions. You could say she draws this out by using herself as a vanishing point for her own writing, just as you do for your paintings.
ML   Interesting! Well, I just draw a line for the mouth. For a few years, I wondered if I should add more – teeth, an open mouth – but something made me resist doing that. I don't know what it is. I've never really said this before, but I wonder if it's a family thing. Especially on my father's side of the family, my sisters and I have a kind of base expression. We go through life straight-faced, with this non-committal line – not an expression as such, but just a line across the face – never severe, maybe slightly bemused. That deadpan look prevailed in most of my family photos, and that look is still present in the characters in my current painting. A sort of absolute neutrality but not unobservant. It's the kind of expression you can't put your finger on. In my paintings, I want that to come across. I hope that the figures are conveying that there's somebody in there – that they are characters.

TWR   How much did your upbringing affect your decision to become an artist, and the kind of work that you make?

ML   I was born in Houghton, Michigan. My family moved to Rochester during the Second World War, then to Chicago, and eventually to Gainesville where my father became chair of Electrical Engineering at the University of Florida until his death in 1965. With three daughters, my parents couldn't afford to send us away to college, so I had to live at home for those undergrad years, which at the time felt awful. I had a sort of epiphany at some point, realising that I could take on the challenge of turning my family and home into my subjects, turning what seemed like the banality of my existence into something interesting. As it turned out, this was the determining attitude of my life's work. I took countless photographs of my family, who were great subjects. My father, particularly, could look like an angst-ridden Bergman character or a Victor Borge.

My parents had high standards for my two sisters and me, but seldom pressured us. I never felt destined to be an artist, and even through college I was still debating: piano, acting, art, philosophy, teaching, law, or even science? My sisters and I were actively encouraged to follow our interests, and my parents also always made it clear that being a woman was no obstacle. My mother got her BA in her twenties and got her PhD after my father died when she was 50, then taught at the University of Florida until she was in her mid-70s. Both my grandmothers went to college.

TWR   There's a certain poetry in your choices
of subject matter, especially with the more absurd
subject matter. I'm thinking of your great painting of the biker and chainsaw – *Chainsawer and
Bicyclist* (2014). These are combinations that don't
make particular sense in any kind of real-life context, but they're also immediately recognisable. Do
these paintings also come from looking at a form
in a work, the Rorschach technique you spoke of,
and then translating it? Or is it ever from life?
ML   *Chainsawer and Bicyclist* was based on
Lissitzky's *Proun 19D* (1922). When I'm looking
at Lissitzky, I'm looking for a hidden reading,
and as I'm looking, the hidden thing that I start
to see becomes very real. When I simplified and
translated what I saw, I ended up with a woman
holding a chainsaw, and a bicyclist. The whole situation looked very plausible to me, but I thought,
who's going to believe a chainsawing woman in
a dress? And then it happened – it was one of
those serendipitous things. A friend of mine who
I'd been out of touch with for some years quit
making art and moved to Maine, and out of the
blue she wrote to me and sent me a photograph,
and a message that said: 'I'm loving it here.' And
she's standing in the front yard with a dress on
and a chainsaw. I hadn't finished the painting yet.
Nobody had seen it, and she couldn't have known.
You know, who chainsaws in a dress?

E. M.,
June 2018

WORKS

PLATES

XXVII	*Drawing Hands*, 2017
XXVIII	*Cabinet Meeting (with Coffee)*, 2018
XXIX	*Cabinet Meeting*, 2017
XXX	*Cup Tricks*, 2018
XXXI	*Hand Slap Game*, 2018
XXXII	*Situation Room (Scissors, Rocks, Paper)*, 2018
XXXIII	*Lecture*, 2011
XXXIV	*Board*, 2017
XXXV	*Cabinet Meeting: Study*, 2017
XXXVI	*Situation Room: Explanation*, 2017
XXXVII	*Situation Room: Scissors/Rock/Paper*, 2017
XXXVIII	*Cabinet #2*, 2017
XXXIX	*Situation Room: Oblique*, 2017

ART

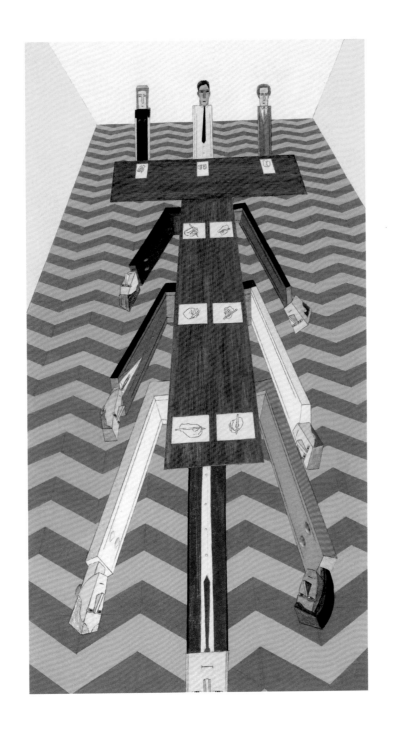

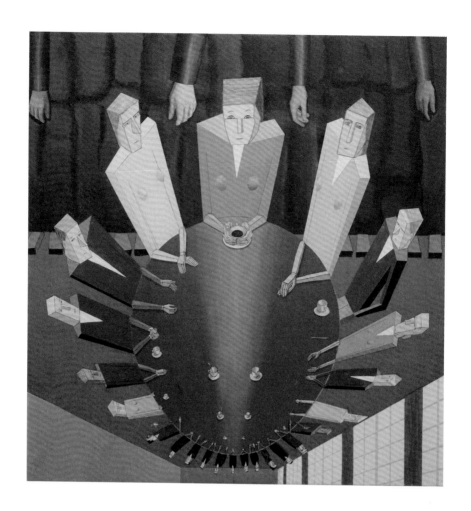

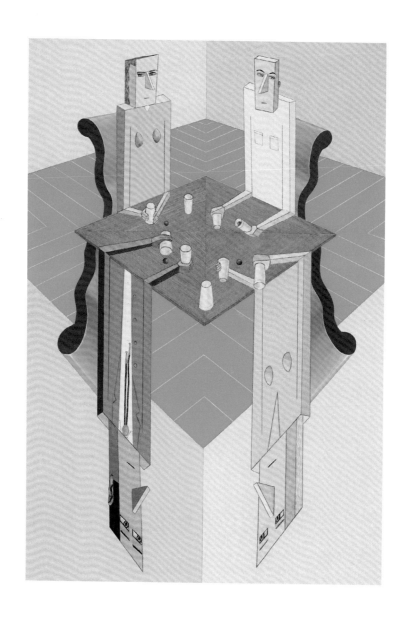

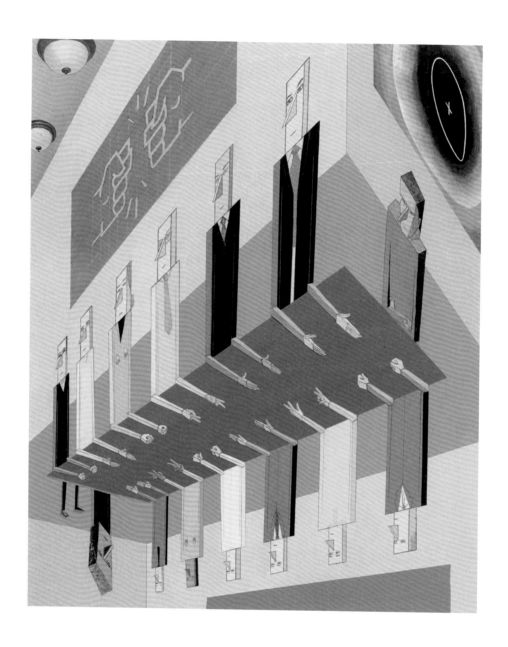

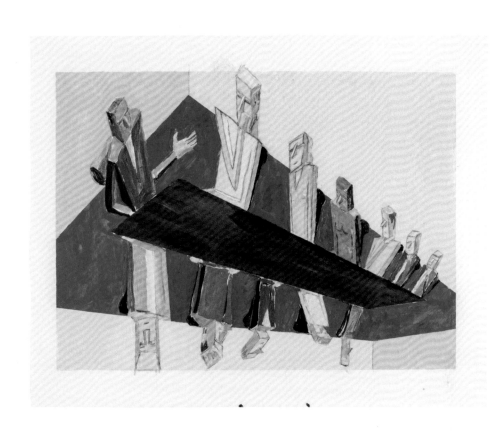

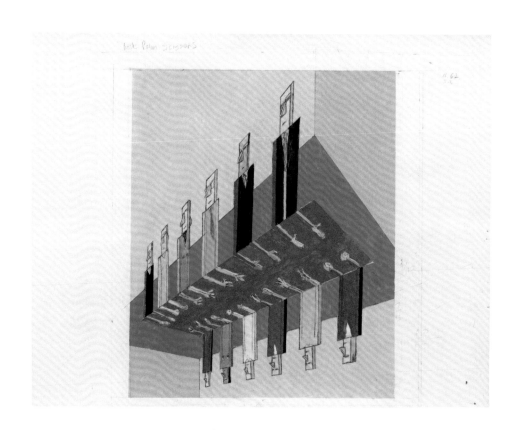

1.

I see your picture for the first time two summers ago, sometime in early July. I am scrolling through Facebook, my forearms hurting from spending too much time at the computer, when I chance upon a picture of you with your arm around a girl I recognise from my time at art school. I am taken by your face, the top half of which is covered by a pair of sunglasses, the bottom with a thick moustache. You are wearing a full sleeve T-shirt, and a pair of headphones hang casually around your notably broad neck. I can't be sure given the fuzzy background, but it looks like you are standing in the middle of a busy marketplace. 'OMG... full lowwww!' someone comments beneath the picture. 'Full loweeeee[1] is right!' you reply. Based on the delight on the girl's face as she looks up at you, delirious from your attention, I assume a romantic bond. I am jealous of her happiness, of her ability to hold you and look at you the way she does, in a way that I imagine I will never be able to.

I remember first encountering your photograph while sitting in my bedroom in my old family house in West Delhi, by the window overlooking the large sports complex with the cricket field and newly built swimming pool. But this cannot be right. Your photograph was uploaded on 2 July, 2016, well after my parents and I had relocated to their current house in North Delhi, in late 2013. I remember the first time I saw a series of pornographic magazines was in that old house, on a summer's day in August 1995. Perhaps this is why my memory plays tricks on me, for I have since returned to your picture with the same furtive image-lust. That day in '95 I skipped school, pretending to be sick so that I could re-watch three video cassettes I had found in the TV cupboard some months earlier, none of which were explicit per se, but all of which contained a few scenes that kept me sexually invested for a short period of time. *All the Right Moves* (1983), an American college football movie starring Tom Cruise, and *The Piano* (1993), Jane Campion's romantic tale of a mute musician, were stored in the third drawer. *Color of Night* (1994), an erotic thriller with Bruce Willis, was in another cupboard, stored carefully under a stack of my father's official university papers and a box of condoms. Of these three, the one I watched most frequently was *All the Right Moves*, always returning to a lovemaking scene between Cruise and Lea Thompson somewhere around the one-hour mark. It includes close-up shots of their nipples grazing as she removes her slip, a long shot of him undoing his Jesus necklace and placing it in his jeans pocket, and finally – this one was my favourite – a blink-and-you-miss-it shot of his crotch as he takes off his jeans.

While rummaging through my parents' bedroom in the hope of finding further material, I discovered the magazines inside a brown paper bag in their safe, under a stack of fresh bank notes and my mother's gold jewellery. The bag had become thin over time, and I made a gash in the paper in my haste to explore its contents: *Penthouse*, *Debonair*, and two Spanish magazines which I assume were bought by my father during his year as an exchange fellow at a business school in Barcelona in 1989. In the years since, when I have tried to imagine him buying the magazines, I picture the expressions of anxious excitement on the faces of the young men who lurk around the magazine stalls in Connaught Place, hoping not to be recognised as they peer at the assortment. I wonder if my father was ever one of them.

1. Informal way of saying 'love'.

One of the photo stories in the Spanish magazines featured a woman astride a motorbike with her legs spread, inside a studio recreation of a graffiti-splattered men's loo. Her femininity was amplified by her submission to objects with which heterosexual men can easily identify: the large, black motorbike and fresh graffiti which drips on her as she places one foot on a urinal for support. As a 12-year-old boy confused by his attraction to men, I felt a mixture of nervousness and confusion looking at her genitalia. It was only after flipping through many pages that I finally saw a man, standing next to a queen-sized bed, opposite a woman in lace lingerie. He is wearing a white shirt and black trousers, and his sharp Hispanic features, tanned skin, muscular, hairy body and blow-dried hair made him look like Julio Iglesias (notorious, at the time, for announcing that he had had sex with more than 3,000 women). As the storyboard proceeds the pair inch their way towards each other, shedding their clothes in the process, until the woman inserts his penis first into her mouth, then her vagina, and finally her ass. I carefully scanned the images into my brain, adding them to an already-large mental archive for my planned weekly masturbation sessions. Now, as if guided by a private compulsion, when I am alone I return over and again to your picture on Facebook, as I once returned to Tom Cruise, and later to the Spanish man. On one such visit, I note that the photograph was taken in the midday sun, causing the girl from art school to squint one of her eyes. You look down calmly, your sunglasses hiding your face from the bright light. She has used a pencil to tie her hair into a bun – an art school trope. Everything you wear is blue.

2.

The night before I encounter you in person for the first time, I cancel going to 'Step Inside and You are No Longer a Stranger', the opening of a large museum retrospective of Vivan Sundaram's work at the Kiran Nadar Museum of Art, at the last minute. It is early February, the beginning of art fair week in Delhi, the air is thick with smog, and the city clogged with openings, parties and collateral events. The retrospective opens on the day I come back from an artist residency in Pune, and I am exhausted: too many artists, too much drama, too much theorising about art-making. I avoid picking up a friend's calls for a while but cave in on his fourth attempt and pretend to be in bed. The next day I spend listlessly flicking through YouTube videos of drag queens giving make-up tutorials, and Tumblr pages dedicated to beefy Indian men.

My desktop is demarcated by sixteen folders, all of which contain links to the websites I frequent. Among them are DAILY, DOWN-LOAD, ART, JOB, READ LATER, CAMERA, BUY, BODY, and MUSIC. Right in the bottom corner is X, in which I store a record of my favourite pornographic websites and Tumblr pages, and a few saved videos. A sub-folder of X titled 'Desi'[2] contains a list of Tumblr pages of big-bodied, middle- and lower-class Indian men: Shuddhdesi[3] men,

2. A loose term for the people, cultures, and products of the Indian diaspora, derived from the ancient Sanskrit term for 'land' or 'country'. The term is fairly loose and thus fairly subjective, but it is widely accepted that India, Pakistan and Bangladesh are Desi countries.
3. 'Shuddh': pure, undiluted.
4. 'Jaat': originally meaning 'tribe', but specifically referring to a specific tribe of people from Punjab in north India.

sexyjaat,[4] Matured Indian Bear, sexydesimen, Indian muscular man, desi gay stuff, sexy desi hunk, SMOKIN HOT INDIAN MEN. The images and videos that excite me are hard and brutish, and I turn to them during days of emptiness and frustration, as a violent juncture from the suffocating pressures of solitude and deadlines. Masculine violence, and the fetishisation of the lower class, are problems I frequently discuss with my queer friends. Knowing it to be anathema to my politics, and afraid of being judged for wanting what I also publicly critique, I keep this line of desire secret.

I may be ashamed, but I am not alone. Perhaps the rise of nationalism, with its fantasy of bloody masculinity and constant threat of violence, has infected the collective sexual psyche; perhaps the disjuncture between the cleanliness of queer ethics and the baseness of desire has sent more people like me in search of amoral material; perhaps heterosexuality dominates and excludes queer men so much that our subjugation has become our fetish; perhaps internet-sexuality, a mode of desire that revolves around abuses of power and easy typecasting, has simply continued to extend its dominion. Whatever the reasons, since 2017 there has been an increase in the number of amateur videos appearing on these India-specific Tumblr pages, and most of them follow a similar trajectory. A camera is placed upon a table, positioned below the waist of the protagonist in order to make him appear larger; the subject flexes his biceps, moves his hand up and down his penis, and smiles as he does a full turn to show you the results of a carefully crafted gym regime, thriving on the attention of faceless viewers who will get off to this image on their phones and computers. There's usually a television on in the background, creating a soundtrack of news reporters talking frenetically, or commentary from a cricket match with the sound of screaming fans muzzled out, or dialogue from an old Bollywood movie. 'Indian Hunk Jerking Off', a video saved in the sub-folder 'Desi' which I count among my favourites, offers a minor variation on this formula. In it a Punjabi man (verified by his wearing of a kada[5]) of muscular build in his mid-twenties sits on the bathroom floor, on top of a neatly folded pile of clothes that he has removed. The camera phone aids his self-fulfilling prophecy: he wants the online world to honour him as a sexual overlord, and in this film he becomes one. After pressing the record button he gives a quick flex of his arms, once behind his head and again behind his back. Placing his hands on his knees he stares with clear intent at the camera, then breathes deeply as he moves his penis from side to top and finally parallel to the ground. At the 45-second mark, he ejaculates. No bodily actions pre-empt this climax – no contorted features, no opening of mouth, no sound, no rolling of eyes or jerking back of head – just a mild pause and a quick look down to make sure he hasn't soiled the pile of clothes. Ejaculate spills out in eight spurts, each reducing in quantity until the last, which is barely a flicker of a drop. At the 55-second mark he moves towards the phone to press the stop button. The undercurrent of trepidation that laces this video brings me back to it over and again. I search for signs as to the context in which the ritual was recorded, attempting to absorb every detail of the moment this good-looking man's veneer of virile confidence is cracked by his fear of being found out. (Why else worry about dirtying his clothes?) What locality of Delhi does he lives in? Who does his laundry? Are his parents in the next room, as mine often are? His wife?

5. Bangle worn by Punjabi men.

I look at the bathroom in the background and imagine what lies beyond
the door, what he will do after he finishes this recording.

A little past 6 p.m., after trawling through my pornographic archive,
I head out to my usual cruising spots, but nobody piques my interest.
I return home and turn on Grindr, scrolling through a smorgasbord of
blurry faces, well-defined torsos, sunsets, porn stars and local television
and movie stars. The area I live in has a low density of Grindr users so
the boxes usually move up north towards Delhi University where the
young college kids are, a demographic in which I have little interest. After
a while I see a profile I vaguely recognise – a semi-naked torso photographed in evening light, and a hand covering half a face. I'm pretty sure
it is S., the Brazilian yoga teacher from the coffee shop a few years ago.
I message, asking if he remembers.

At 8 p.m., the friend I blew off the previous evening calls again. He's
heading to a photography show called 'Mutations' before the opening
night party, and insists that I hurry and don't arrive late as usual. I open
my cupboard, put on the light purple sweater I bought at H&M last
December, and head to 24, Jor Bagh – a residential bungalow owned by
an ex-supermodel turned wealthy art patron, that has been converted into
a space for art practices which sit outside Delhi's mainstream commercial
gallery circuit. The bungalow has two floors in which a maze of rooms
lead into each other, where the interior walls are a mixture of chipped
paint and carelessly thrown-on cement, all spotlit by expensive track
lighting that carefully choreographs the space's alternative credentials.
'Mutations' is a 'large-scale contemporary exhibition', runs the press
release, 'positing how we envision public and private zones as interlinked
domains of encounter'. As I read the text I do not think of mass-migra-
tion, 'identities in flux', or any of the other grand themes that the exhibition's curators would like me to, nor do I think of Malayalam fairytales
and European settlers, as the artworks would like me to. Instead the
relationship between the 'public' and the 'private' makes me think of how
my desire has become pixelated and secretive; how sexual encounters play
out like gifs and videos, discrete scenes to be stored away in the archive of
memory, sequestered from my social life. 24, Jor Bagh attracts a particular
kind of crowd: young curators and artists with degrees from expensive art
schools in America, the old art frat drinking free booze and talking over
each other, and a smattering of eager, art school kids along with South
Delhi hipsters. There are a number of attractive, heterosexual men present, and one boy in particular who I cannot stop looking at. He is dressed
in that painfully casual manner that straight men sometimes have: short-
cropped hair and soft stubble, loose, ill-fitting jeans, and a baggy sweater
hiding a body that looks like it has endured years of football training.
He's talking to two nondescript Caucasian girls, both of whom look as
enamoured by him as I am. My desire for heterosexuality – the residue of
a childhood yearning for acceptance from something always out of reach
– accompanies me still. Like the image of you on Facebook with a smitten
girl under your arm, his status as an object of desire among women makes
me want him more than I otherwise would. I cannot hear what he's saying but smile at the sight of his large, beautiful arms, which move up and
down animatedly as he speaks.

About an hour later my friends and I head to the party at the Swiss
Embassy that officially kicks off Delhi Art Week, a glitzy affair indic-
ative of the money pumped into the art world at this time of year. We
pass through the security check at the gate, and into a large outdoor
area bisected by a pool I recognise from the opening party the previous

year. Hovering over the pool are a series of large balloons onto which video works by the Swiss artist Katja Loher are projected, in which figures dance in formations that look like wild, blooming flowers. Here, the Delhi art crowd is joined by a few expensive-looking socialites who linger on the sidelines, and a large dollop of white male expatriates, all of whom wear black and blue blazers with formal trousers. Food stands run the length of the pool, the highlight of which is a dessert section with a large chocolate fountain. At the buffet, which includes an assortment of European dishes the names of which I find hard to pronounce, I bump into the boy who dated my ex after me. He is muscular in the way that his clothes stick to his body, demanding that you pay attention, soliciting enquiries about his workout routine. Conversation is awkward, as it always is with him. He backs up questions one after the other with no pause, pushing me to answer in quick succession. Eventually the music gets louder and people head to the dance floor – an elevated stage at the far end of the room. Two years after discovering your photograph online, it is here that I first see you. You are talking to a group of people, most of whom are my friends. Seeing your full body for the first time, there is a vertical tautness to you that I've noticed in trained basketball players. You are wearing a padded brown jacket on top of a crisp white shirt and khaki pants. When a mutual friend introduces us I say 'Hey' and quickly look away. I am nervous in your presence, and as we exchange light and inconsequential conversation I struggle to make eye contact. The music slows down to Prince's 'Purple Rain', and you put your arm on my shoulder and ask if I'd like a male or female dancing partner. Because I've assumed a romantic relationship between you and the girl from art school, I take you for a straight man and your question for a taunt. The moment triggers memories from high school of boys making casual jokes about my lack of interest in girls; I shake my head with discomfort and move away. On the way home my friend asks why I did not reciprocate your interest in me, and I am dismayed to discover my mistake, forced to acknowledge that aged 35 I have needlessly turned a fantasy into a tired, teenage nightmare.

3.
In an attempt to rectify the situation I get your number from the friend who introduced us, and send you a WhatsApp message the next day, Saturday 10 February, 2018 at 3.39 p.m. I draft it six times to make sure I don't sound too eager. After introducing myself, I ask if you'd like to meet. 'Was wondering if you'd like to grab a coffee today? If you're in Delhi that is.' You reply three hours later, and to my excitement you tell me that you have to meet a few friends, but are free afterwards. We decide to head to the mall for coffee, where to my surprise we spend most of our time together fielding earnest questions from the other. I'm conscious that sincerity has replaced the mood of flirtation I failed to recognise the night before. You have a formality to you that is notably different in the light of the coffee shop, and you ask me about my childhood, my time at art school, and my ex-boyfriends. As we prepare to part I tell you that I am heading to a friend's place and ask if you'd like to join, but you mention an early morning flight and politely decline. My disappointment at this is tempered by a sense of elation at our meeting; I leave hopeful about where this could lead.

Between 10 February and 5 March, my hope is fanned as we exchange twenty-six pictures on WhatsApp. Of these, seven are sent by you and nineteen by me. Of the seven you send, two are selfies, the first with the friend who introduced us. In the picture you are sitting at a table, with your hand around what looks like a beer bottle. Both of you are looking down towards the camera, and given the angle of your left shoulder I'm guessing it is you who is holding the phone. At 6.22 p.m. on Monday 19 February, after you tell me that you have been working on your 'shoulders and abs today', you send me the second selfie. It shows you flexing your right arm with an outward-facing fist; in your left hand you are holding a silver iPhone a little below eye level. As you perform for your audience you do not kneel on a neatly folded pile of clothes like the star of 'Indian Hunk Jerking Off', yet there are other clues to be gleaned about your life and attitude: two large windows, a dressing table with a mirror on top of it, cupboards made from expensive wood, and your sizeable, disheveled bed, fill a room in what looks like a typical suburban house. The sheets are a pastel shade of pink, and on top of them lies a blanket in a deep shade of blue.

On Monday 5 March, somewhere between 10.30 and 11 p.m., I get back on Facebook after a fourteen-month hiatus, specifically to skim through your pictures. It is the longest I have spent away from the social network, a break necessitated by an overwhelming anxiety about my life, career and finances that snowballed after my day job ended in December 2016, leaving me without reliable employment. Two weeks after I return, the *New York Times* and the *Observer* release information proving that Facebook has shared the data of more than 87 million users with Cambridge Analytica, a political consulting firm that was employed by the Trump presidential campaign. A furore ensues about privacy, and about how much of ourselves we share online. But I think about how little I am able to know about you despite scrolling through thousands of your pictures. You have twenty-six photo albums on your Facebook profile. The total sum of photographs in these albums is 1,066. Seventy-two of these are from your profile pictures album. Of these seventy-two, five do not have you in them. Thirty-four include other people, and six have other people cropped out of the frame. All show you at ease with the camera, excited to be photographed, chronicled and added to a large database of collective memories online. A photograph uploaded on Thursday 14 July 2016 has gained 200 likes, the most of all your pictures. It shows you sitting on the steps of a local, South Indian bus with a bag on your back and camera in hand. You are wearing a checked shirt, black pants and brown leather shoes. The focus of all the commentary around the picture is your moustache. It is the kind that has been curled at the ends, mostly seen on burly security guards outside expensive hotels. 'This handlebar is serious,' one friend says. 'What's with the pornstache?' another asks. The blue seats and green steps of the bus add balance to the deep red of your shirt. As I sift carefully through your pictures, I find a photograph taken on the dance floor the night we met, uploaded on Friday 17 February. Almost everyone in the picture is a varying degree of blurriness. You are the only one in sharp focus.

4.

Unsure how to read our exchanges to date, I decide to push for a resolution. On Friday 30 March, fifty days after first meeting you at the opening night party, during which time we have met once and exchanged over 2,000 messages, I take an overnight bus to Bangalore, the city where you live. I have arranged to stay with the friend who introduced us, after carefully planning with him to make sure you will also be free. The alibi for my unannounced visit: a Saturday afternoon lunch with artists and curators visiting from Europe. The bus ride is over 900 kilometres and takes a little more than fifteen hours. I arrive at my friend's apartment early to help prepare the food. When you finally appear at lunch my excitement at seeing you is quickly tempered: there is an awkwardness between us that dampens the atmosphere of sexual provocation which I had read into our exchange of photographs.

After lunch the rest of the guests leave, but you decide to stick around. The three of us watch the first episode of *The Assassination of Gianni Versace: American Crime Story*, and I put my hand on your right knee, only to have you immediately brush it off and move beyond my reach. The rest of the afternoon is spent planning what to do and where to go that evening, and I am distracted by the mounting realisation that this trip may have been a mistake. We decide to head to a brewery and then on to a gay party at The Sugar Factory, a nightclub at a fancy hotel later that evening. In an attempt to play Cupid, our mutual friend suggests that you spend the night at his place so that three of us can go out together again the day after. There is talk of swimming at the pool, or even heading out of the city for a long drive, but nothing is finalised.

By the time we arrive at the club, you have grown cold and aloof. From the bar I watch you mill about in the crowds, looking at men looking at you, your chest and head raised in the way men hold themselves when they are putting on a front for other men. Back at the apartment later that night, my friend insists that he will sleep on the couch in the front room, so that you and I can share his bedroom. Despite all evidence to the contrary, I hold out hope that you might let your guard down when we are completely alone together for the first time that day. Instead you sniffle and cough your way through an allergy attack, recoiling on the bed so that your body is as far from mine as possible. I ask you what's going on, why I'm getting such mixed signals, why you seem so different in person. You tell me that this is new for you, that you're not ready, that you have only been interested in older men, men in their fifties, that when we first met you felt a connection that was unusual because it is rare for you to feel anything for someone like me.

In the morning I roll over to look at you, hoping that in the few hours between our dispiriting conversation and now you might have magically changed your mind, moved your body closer to mine so that I can smell your morning breath, laugh with familiarity and affection, tell me that you've made a mistake, that this is to you what it is to me. Instead you are curled up with your eyes shut and your handkerchief still in hand. I wonder if this is a front, if the handkerchief is merely a way of letting me know that I should steer clear of your face. Your body is in a foetal position, soft silk basketball shorts accentuating your already prominent ass. The band of your white underwear sticks out and I imagine what it would feel like to touch it. What would it smell like, your sweaty, used underwear close to my mouth as I peel it off and have you face down while I eat your ass until spit is falling onto the sheets, making large pools that lay bare my desire for you. I like when a boy moans gently as I stick my tongue in there, increasing the pace as both of us start gliding in similar motion towards each other, his ass moving closer to my tongue, my tongue digging deeper into his hole. I wonder if you would make any noise, whether you would grunt or moan, whether your face would contort if some of your ass hair gets stuck between my teeth, whether you would make eye contact or keep your eyes shut if I turn you over and pull your legs up so I can see how you respond to each flick of my tongue.

Restless, deflated and unable to watch you as you sleep, I decide to take a walk. I look at you from the doorway before I leave and see you

as a photograph, an image once in fine detail that is losing texture and
fading before my eyes. Once outside I shut the gate behind me and head
onto the main road, walking past a half-broken-down house, an empty
church that in a few hours will be filled with worshippers celebrating the
end of Lent with Easter Sunday mass, past the guard at the big apartment
complex about to finish his night duty, past a cute Doberman and his lady
owner who shifts across the pavement when I walk by, past the super-
market where my friend and I bought food for the lunch we made for you
yesterday afternoon. When I get back, you are just getting out of bed.
After a bath, you decide to take a walk yourself and ask if I would like to
join you. I say no: the idea of making conversation now seems impossibly
laborious. When you leave the house, I switch on Grindr hoping for
a distraction. The closest square I see on the grid was last online 21 minutes ago. 'I am mainly interested in older men and a muscular or beefy
body definitely garners my attention. However, just be height/weight
proportionate. If you are able to hold a conversation – that's a bonus! Dp
is mine.' Your picture is fairly nondescript. All that is visible is your torso
leading into what looks like a pair of tracksuit bottoms with a thin band
of boxers visible above the waistline. There is a brown towel in the left
hand side of the image, and a strong tan line on your right arm. I look at
the size of your arms and compare them to mine. *Muscular* and *beefy* ring
in my head, louder and louder, like one of those German electronic tracks
I sometimes listen to at the gym. This time the rhythm is jarring, like thin
paper cutters on a chalkboard, cancelling out whatever little hope I had
with you.

ON CLASS ROUNDTABLE

How do we begin to talk about class in the UK? Class shapes the structures of our society, influences and is influenced by policy. It intersects, absolutely, with race, gender, sexuality and disability. It filters into our everyday interactions, our relationships and aspirations, mediating the reality of our lived experiences. So, where do we start? Perhaps with data. In 2013, the BBC, with Professors Fiona Devine and Mark Savage, conducted the Great British Class Survey, gathering information from 160,000 participants about the amount and kind of economic, cultural and social capital they possess – a framework based on Pierre Bourdieu's theory of social distinction. Analysing the data, seven class categories were identified – the precariat sit at the 'bottom', with the least of all types of capital, and the elite sit at the 'top', with the most. Mapped, the results are stark, but not surprising: there were far more elites in the south than the north.

We could instead talk more concretely about socioeconomics. Over the past several years, the Equality and Human Rights Commission has gathered data to analyse the cumulative impact of the austerity reforms initiated by the Coalition government in 2010 and continued by the majority, now minority, Tory governments. The Commission's final report, published this March, confirms what many have either suspected or actually lived through: unquestionably, the poorest suffer most from austerity. For households with at least one disabled adult and a disabled child, average annual cash losses under austerity will be over 13 per cent of average net income; the greatest economic losers from the reforms are disabled women of (what the Commission classify as) 'Mixed ethnicity' and 'Other' ethnic groups. Austerity, the Commission concludes, is regressive. But how much does socioeconomic data tell us about class? In a 2012 interview, cultural theorist Stuart Hall said that 'there is is no permanent, fixed class-consciousness. You can't work out immediately what people think and what politics they have simply by looking at their socioeconomic position.' Figures can flatten out details. Data tells us little about the lived reality of our class-defined society – about the corrosive sense of guilt and betrayal that can accompany the moving from one ill-defined class to another; about the experience of witnessing, firsthand, the rapid and irreversible gentrification of your community.

In this roundtable, we talk about our own encounters with class-consciousness, as well as the concept of hard work and its relation to artistic practice. We talk about class-as-aesthetic, the insidiousness of class codes – learning or not learning 'how to play the game' – and the language surrounding recent inclusivity drives in the arts. London features heavily – as a narrative of potential capitalist success, as a site of unending gentrification, and as a capital that coexists uneasily with the rest of the country. We touch on Brexit, tracksuits and streetlights. Despite the multifaceted nature of this conversation, it remains a product of five individuals. While it is our intent that each roundtable act as a conversation starter – rather than as the final word – we feel that the scope and complexities of the subject warrant further discussions, writings and perhaps events, featuring a breadth of voices from different generations, geographic backgrounds and artistic practices. Consider this roundtable the beginning of a wider exploration into class.

RALF WEBB   Discussions around class tend to involve, sooner or later, everyone stating their own class background, and qualifying the discussion in a personal way. Do you think that this is the only way we can ever talk about class, and does every conversation about class necessarily have to be personal?
MATTHEW SPERLING   It makes sense to me that discussions would come back to the personal, because of the sense that class isn't just a set of socio-economic facts, but is also partly in the head. It's one's experiences of those facts, and it's how those experiences create meanings in the world.
RAYMOND ANTROBUS   That question is really, 'are we compassionate?' And as a culture I don't know if we are. I've lived in a few different countries and that's often something I think about: people here are compassionate, or here people are able to express something that is difficult to express. I think that class is part of the British mentality or British history, and because it's a thing that we're skilled in talking about, class is the thing that's the most —
WEBB   It intersects with absolutely everything.
ANTROBUS   Exactly, yeah.
WEBB   But do you think we are skilled in talking about it? To me, there seems to be a reticence or hesitance to actually engage with the issue and to talk about it openly.
AYO AKINGBADE   I wish class was an illusion. I identify as working-class and my family are not in the arts, so for me to pursue work in the industry, I've had to do it by myself, and when I'm talking to important art people, clearly there's a way that I speak that's different. You can definitely tell someone is from a working-class background by the way they speak, and that makes a big difference as you move into new circles. I think it's something that's in the fabric of our society, it's not going to change and it's always going to be personal.
ANTROBUS   I've been working in a deaf school and I speak some sign language and it's so fascinating to me how even in that space there's a refined, elaborate sign, and then there's a working-class, more abbreviated sign. So class even plays out in that, it has an expression.
SPERLING   I feel like that aspect of how class plays out in Britain can sometimes obfuscate the discussion. The sense that class is actually about mannerisms, whether you crook your finger when you drink your tea, all this Downton Abbey stuff. Sometimes I think it gets in the way of

the economic, material truth being looked at, as though class is just about whether you call it your 'tea' or your 'dinner', or whatever. But that's really interesting that even in a totally different language you have the same sort of distinctions.
TESS DENMAN-CLEAVER   The pervasiveness of class — and I don't have a lot of experience of other cultures particularly, so I mean the pervasiveness of class in the UK — means that there's not a part of my day that isn't experienced through class in some way. And the other side of that is that I'm always really aware of what my contribution to — and this also relates to this conversation — a conversation is. I've come down from Newcastle today and I was immediately trying to second-guess the selection process for this conversation. Like, am I the token northerner? And then I think, am I northern enough, and is northern working-class? I'm always aware of my value in that kind of dynamic — which is not necessarily a relatively formalised conversation like this one — but in any kind of conversation, with peers from university or working in the arts. I'm always incredibly aware of what my identity presents. And sometimes I think it's deceiving.
WEBB   Deceiving in what way?
DENMAN-CLEAVER   I've been thinking a lot about how someone's class is presented. Actually, I think that through various circumstances my class is not particularly identifiable. But I'm still really aware of what I bring to a conversation and what everybody else may bring, or what their perspective might be according to what I have presumed their social status to be. I just couldn't see a way of having this conversation without talking about the statistics as an experience of everyday life. Even data on class is understood through a personal lens, like, 'Oh I'm that per cent working class' or, 'I haven't had that experience' or, 'I have had that'.

LANGUAGE;
'STATUS INCONGRUITY'

ANTROBUS   I think that ultimately it's about education. I've worked a lot in schools — I didn't have a very conventional education but now I'm a poet who works in schools, and for some time I was trying to work out if I was betraying myself because I'm now endorsing an environment that didn't serve me, that I didn't prosper in. There's definitely a class anxiety within me because I would say I grew up working-class, but a few years back my sister — who was the first one in my family to finish university — said to me, 'You know we're middle-class now?' and I remember in that moment being like, 'Oh.'

WEBB   How do you feel about that?

ANTROBUS   To link it back to what we were saying before about language, I think there is a working-class language, and I feel like now — because I've learnt it, I've been through it — I'm quite well-versed in middle-class language, and I appreciate that I've been able to cohabit both of those spaces. But there's still an anxiety that I feel in both of those spaces about belonging. There's still this feeling of, 'Maybe I'm being judged or there's some way that I have to assert something, I have to do some coded thing', and it's constant.

SPERLING   One of the things which made most sense to me on that subject was a book by Richard Sennett called *The Hidden Injuries of Class*, it's a book of radical sociology. His study is about American people who have left the working class and have been the beneficiaries of class mobility, have become white-collar workers, have become property owners and all that. It's about the psychic wounds of that position, of what he calls the 'status incongruity' of being in a social position that isn't the one you occupied growing up. You constantly feel a lack of legitimacy, and lack sources of dignity in your life. And that made a lot of sense to me. I mean, the sort of social distance I've had to travel to be someone who writes books and teaches at university is not very far, it's a very minor kind of class displacement, but still it's enough that it makes sense to me as well.

ANTROBUS   I just want to speak about that condition of having internal tensions. I'm so used to that tension as well — I think that it's almost just part of my being. I mean in the sense of growing up Jamaican and British, and growing up deaf and hearing. I went to a deaf school and a hearing school and I was so lucky to have the NHS because I got ten years of speech therapy, hearing therapy, my own counsellor, in-class support, all of it free of charge. Which is amazing, because at the end of the day I was going back to a council flat. It's something that I do think about a lot actually, the fact that I had that, that form of privilege. It feels like such an injustice because this year £4 million was cut from deaf education services, and recently some of the oldest deaf schools in the country were shut down. It doesn't make any sense, at the moment you have a rising number of people being

born deaf and fewer avenues for them to get the support I received. That's also an internal tension that plays out when I work in schools — deaf or hearing — and I see someone who has a need which I recognise and I want to be able to help them, but you need an infrastructure, I can't do it on my own. That's one reason I had to step back from teaching in schools, I couldn't look after myself. I was trying to do too much and the system was just failing.

AKINGBADE   I'm from Hackney in East London, I was born and went to school there. But when I went to film school in South London, everything changed. I became the minority. Class was such a big aspect of university and I didn't expect that. I just wanted to be a filmmaker and meet like-minded people and it was a big shock. My first year I was quite depressed because I couldn't navigate that world, I didn't know how or what I could do or how I could be successful in it.

My aim in any piece I create is to delve into issues I think are not showcased in the mainstream, questions that aren't usually seen in film from a black woman's point of view. One reason I decided to make my film *Tower XYZ* (2016) was because I was frustrated with a certain dogma taught on my BA course. I felt it didn't give me space to create pieces about my culture. Films surrounding class and gentrification were essentially taboo. And now, Elephant and Castle, where I studied, is changing at a rapid pace — the shopping centre is going to be demolished to allow 979 homes and a new university campus. We will definitely lose the ethnic community hubs that once were for what — profit?

WEBB   Why do you think that films about class and gentrification weren't encouraged on your BA?

AKINGBADE   I didn't do an art foundation, so I didn't have the opportunity to mingle with other young, eager artists figuring out what they wanted to do. At university I thought I would meet people who dressed like me, spoke about art passionately and believed in the possibility of changing the world via making films. Class was something I discovered at university because injustice and inequality were right next to me, working hand in hand. I was the only black girl in my class and my life experience was quite different to others. I felt that the stories that were supported were more like fantasy, obscure sci-fi stories. Making fiction was something that was really encouraged.

UNIVERSITY;
CLASS-CONSCIOUSNESS

DENMAN-CLEAVER My experience of going to university was really quite a brutal encounter with class. Though it had been slightly prefaced by moving out of the city and going to a posh state school and dropping my Geordie accent to survive.
WEBB Was this at Trinity College?
DENMAN-CLEAVER Yeah, in Dublin. I had a massive amount of prejudice, like as far as I was concerned private schools were evil, and if you went there you were complicit in some kind of social injustice, rather than your parents just sent you there, just like my parents sent me to my school. And it took me ages to make any friends, though I made really good friends eventually. I remember in Freshers' Week people kept asking me what school I'd gone to and they all knew the names of each others' schools. So I said, 'Queen Elizabeth High School?', like is this some weird niche hobby that these people have where they know the names of all the schools in the country? But that's because I didn't know what Westminster School was, I don't think I even knew what Eton was.
SPERLING Going to university was probably the birth of class-consciousness for me. I found myself discovering this world of people with all these social manners and networks and resources that I didn't have. And probably for a period I was then falsely, in this way of internalising the resentment, thinking of myself as much less privileged than I really am...
DENMAN-CLEAVER Yeah yeah yeah.
SPERLING ...of playing up what an underdog I was in Oxford. My dad was a fucking head-teacher! But that movement was quite formative for me. Having grown up where your dad's a teacher and your mum's a librarian, you're actually quite posh in Gravesend, so you're kind of alienated at that end, but then you go to Oxford and suddenly there's all these amazingly rich people, and then you're alienated both ways.
DENMAN-CLEAVER And then the violence of that encounter. I don't think that education-based encounter with class ever goes away. You never lose that constant measuring of whether you're the same or not, or the impulse to hide who your parents are.
WEBB I had a similar experience going to Durham University, which was quite shocking

for me. What was interesting about Durham is that Durham's heritage is as a very working-class town with a mining history. The 'town and gown' divide was very strong. I remember making friends with some locals there and one of them said to me, 'You're posh because you come from the south'. That guy was probably from a wealthier background than I was, but there was that interesting divide, which again goes back to codes.
DENMAN-CLEAVER There is that idea that the north is working-class and the south is posh, and in the north it's really great to be working-class and everyone down south is a soft southerner. Quite often it's glossed over that there are equivalent situations or similar demographics in both places.
ANTROBUS I have a friend who's a professor in neuroscience and he's recently done a survey looking at prejudice. He showed me his findings and it was quite fascinating because the number one most shared prejudice of people in the UK and the States — I don't know how large the case study was but he said it was quite a big study — was major corporations, number two was rich people or posh people, and number three was working-class people. I just found that so interesting. I was quite surprised to see working-class people so high up. I told my mum and my sister this and they were like, 'Surely number one should just be men because it nails all of them.' But I think the thing that shocked me most was that reminder, 'People hate working-class people'.

HARD WORK;
EXPECTATION; VALUES

DENMAN-CLEAVER The BBC had that survey that revealed a new scale of seven different classes, and working-class is everybody below what they call the 'established middle class'. But actually if you think about the hatred towards people on benefits or in social housing then obviously that's a really major national prejudice.
WEBB If you're from a lower-middle or working-class background, however we define these terms, there does tend to be this idea that there's an inherent value in hard work, however that work is defined.
ANTROBUS Definitely. I find it difficult to say 'no' to things. Still. I think my mum has this as well, I think that we still have a working-class mentality. I think we still feel like we could lose

anything at any minute, we're that close to the bread line. It's interesting seeing friends who come from wealthier backgrounds and do similar work to me not have those anxieties and be like, 'I say no to everything'. I'm trying to negotiate that because I'm wondering if still having that in me is limiting or stunting my growth in some way.

WEBB   Is there a conflict between your own artistic practices and what you were brought up to believe is of value or of worth?

AKINGBADE   Definitely. My parents are Nigerian and they have this ideology that you have to make a lot of money to be successful. So people become doctors and lawyers. It's a stereotypical thing, I don't know if it's an immigrant thing, but I get it. So for me to be a filmmaker is difficult. People around me say, 'Your work is amazing, your parents should be proud.' They're proud but they're not overly ecstatic because it's a tricky profession, it's up and down all the time. Unless they see me on TV they won't think that I've made it.

ANTROBUS   I have the same thing. I had an immigrant parent, my dad's from Jamaica, and I never told him I was a poet or that it was what I wanted to do because I just didn't have the language for that. He came from Jamaica with high aspirations and he had to navigate all of the madness of this country, the late 50s, 60s, and so I heard a lot of his grievances about how hard he worked but how the system failed him. That narrative is very present in me to this day, there is a class expectation I'm trying to shift. When I started teaching I was able to say to him, 'I'm a teacher' and he was like 'Ah gotcha!', and I never explained the poet thing, even though it's primarily what I'm known for.

SPERLING   I guess there's a difficulty about the nature of writing as work because it doesn't exactly feel like work when you're doing it. There's all sorts of work you have to do as a poet, like answering emails, but actually you can't write poems for that many hours of the day. I find that when I'm writing a novel, even if it's a day when I don't have to teach, I can maybe do three good hours a day. But if I admit that it sounds like I'm a member of the leisure class. It's hard to reconcile that with ideas about workfulness, and whether you're pushing yourself hard enough.

ANTROBUS   One of the things I'm trying to do to combat these anxieties is to have very specific ideas of success which are only mine. I've realised that in London, or in any city, the environment

you're in is so competitive and you often operate under the assumption that everyone wants to achieve the same thing. But actually when it comes down to it, when you're specific in your goals, you realise they're pretty different to anyone else's and often there is a space for your specific skill and talent and voice. It doesn't need to be like, excuse the expression, crabs in a bucket.

DENMAN-CLEAVER   Jake Berry is the Minister for the Northern Powerhouse and there was this big uproar recently because BAE Systems [an aircraft and arms manufacturer] were funding this 'The Great Exhibition of the North' festival and eventually enough artists said 'We'll drop out if BAE Systems doesn't.' Berry responded on Twitter by saying something like, 'What these subsidy-addicted artists need to realise is that it's the people who work for BAE Systems who pay their bills.' It just really encapsulated the role that culture is required to play, and the lack of respect for it as work or contribution. The other side of that is that BAE Systems is government-funded, so it is also subsidy-addicted.

WEBB   Recently there's been a big push in literature and visual arts organisations to increase diversity in the arts, particularly through funding and funding initiatives. Part of that has included taking into account class background. So, for instance, the publisher Penguin dropped the requirement to have a university degree, and they have quotas and targets to adequately represent the nation as a whole. What do you think about these inclusivity drives?

DENMAN-CLEAVER   One of the things that the Penguin programme includes, if I'm right, is really, really basic, and that is that internships are paid. I mean it's obvious, there's no way most people can't afford to live in London and work unpaid. I think there are more complicated aspects to it, but that's just really basic. You're not going to get anyone else in if you don't pay them.

WEBB   How much have you all encountered that in your own practices — the assumption that you can just work for free?

AKINGBADE   When I was younger I was really into fashion. I did lots of internships which weren't paid and that was just a thing deemed normal, and you were supposed to appreciate the opportunity and network like crazy. I did work experience at a magazine and I asked the editor, 'How can I succeed in the industry?' and she said, 'You have to play the game'. And I was so confused, I was like

'What is the game?' and she just smiled. Yeah, but what is this game? I'm still confused.

My work is about working-class identity, Black Britishness and social housing and most of it is funded by public funds and grants so I'm really appreciative of that. My first commission was via the ICA, Arts Council and Channel 4, and the film wouldn't have happened without that funding. And I don't think I'd be where I am now if I hadn't made that film. So I find it really important, I think those quotas need to exist, but at the same time, it does verge on tokenism. There's a sense of, 'There's this person doing really well, so we're going to support her', but what about the other artists?

'I THINK I MIGHT BE SPECIFIC RATHER THAN DIVERSE'

ANTROBUS   The problem lies with assuming what somebody's most important identity is. Being a son is a very important identity to me, being a cyclist is also a very important identity to me. Race is a whole strange thing but being British-Jamaican and the ways all those things play out is complicated. Tokenism and exoticism are dangerous games.

I think one of my favourite examples is from when I was running a workshop for English teachers. A white English teacher had written a poem about going to India and seeing a Bengal Tiger. She wrote about how it was fiery and beautiful, and she used the word 'exotic' to describe it. There was an Indian-British teacher in the room who said, 'You know the funny thing about how you described that tiger and used the word exotic is that you never realised the danger you might be in.' These assumptions of what is important are dangerous for everyone.

DENMAN-CLEAVER   I'm interested in the danger of tokenism. Initially I was really, really sceptical about the Arts Council Creative Case for Diversity scheme, which collects data and categorises people and their engagement with art on an individual basis. And now I've changed my mind a bit because I think the data that was collected in their survey, which I didn't contribute to because I was so sceptical, means that the sector can actually see itself for the first time, and then start to implement these programmes, as difficult as they are and as complicated as they are.

There's that really amazing Arts Emergency report on diversity in the arts, 'Panic! Social Class, Taste and Inequalities in the Creative Industries'. It just shows you who isn't there. Actually, while I was still really angry about the Creative Case stuff I called up the Arts Council about some fund they were offering. I was trying to work out if it was the right fund for the project I was developing and they asked this really weird question, which then made me really interested in the language of it all. They said to me, 'Are you diverse?'

WEBB   What does that mean?

DENMAN-CLEAVER   I was like, I think I might be specific rather than diverse. But now it's become a way of saying, 'Do you fit into one of our categories that we need more people in?' Instead of saying, are you white or not, are you from a working-class background or not, are you disabled or not? Because they can't ask you those questions, they don't want to. That conversation isn't happening explicitly, and because of that I think the language around it is really interesting.

WEBB   The word 'diverse' is used as a blanket term to cover lower income, to cover race, to cover sexuality, all of those things. Sometimes you're reading a text – a grant application or project description – and it doesn't even make sense.

ANTROBUS   I genuinely feel like the people with power don't have the language to speak to the conversation they're trying to have, meaningfully. Again, having spent time in the States, I was so impressed with a lot of the discourse that's happening there. Particularly around whiteness, what whiteness is and how to unpack whiteness. In the UK, we don't have someone like Tim Wise, a white historian who gives these incredible lectures on the history of European empires, and the invention of whiteness.

DENMAN-CLEAVER   I was thinking about what you were saying earlier Ralf, that people don't talk about class. I don't think that's true. It really is talked about in Newcastle, it's a really everyday language. There's a real, tangible shared experience of not being in the elite. It's not difficult to talk about because it's familiar. But the language around diversity has become completely oblique and confused.

JOBCENTRES; TRACKSUITS

WEBB   I want to talk a little about class as aesthetic. That's something that, for me anyway, was particularly rooted in my experience of coming to London. I started noticing things, like at Cos they sell worker's jackets for £120. You start going to literature events in Working Men's clubs and you're in this space that you know has a particular history and heritage but your experience of it is that it's being used by a bunch of rich, mostly white kids who are super trendy, some of whom are wearing clothes based on designs of clothes worn by the working classes.

ANTROBUS   In Deptford in south-east London there's this place that was a Jobcentre for fifty years. Deptford is now a very complicated area given its history. At one point, a hundred years ago, it was very prosperous, the equivalent of Oxford Street. As time has gone by it's become more and more run-down. Until recently it was very poor, and it's on its way up again now because of gentrification. The Jobcentre closed down for about six months and when it opened again it was a bar. It's still called the Jobcentre but now it's a hipster bar and they've actually kept the original chairs and desks as a kind of aesthetic.

DENMAN-CLEAVER   Why would anyone who's actually been to a Jobcentre want to go to a bar there?

ANTROBUS   We're talking about exoticism again, the fetishising of an experience. Something like the Jobcentre bar is very specific to Britain. That doesn't happen in Jamaica, I can't imagine it happening in any other place I've lived. So, I wonder how much that has to do with whiteness and just sheer arrogance and, going back to the beginning of our conversation, lack of compassion. That is such a clear expression for me of a lack of compassion, because the language is impoverished too.

WEBB   But why is it fetishised? Is it because there's an assumption that there's something authentic about the working classes that can't be accessed by other groups?

DENMAN-CLEAVER   But does it not simultaneously hold it at a distance? Going for a drink in a Jobcentre and enjoying the aesthetic of a Jobcentre makes it quite clear that you will never be in a Jobcentre. You haven't been to sign on or to get your Universal Credits assessment. I don't think it's so much about respect, maybe there is a sort of romanticisation there...

WEBB   Another example is the trend for sportswear, which has become high fashion: you get expensive designer brands emulating designs of classic sportswear, tracksuits essentially. Tracksuits and sportswear mean so many different things to so many different communities — in my hometown, for instance, they had associations with white working-class communities.

ANTROBUS   It's interesting because it can still be an assertion of class. It's like Stormzy being able to wear a really expensive tracksuit, to say I can still go to the ends but I can also...

AKINGBADE   ...go to Chelsea, where I live now.

ANTROBUS   There's something about the uniform that represents that crossover, it's about being able to say, 'I can afford my new life, and I don't have to look different.' It's about asserting a class position that links back to his working-class life.

DENMAN-CLEAVER   I was just thinking back to what you were saying, Ray, about needing to signify your belonging both in a working-class environment and your now middle-class work environment. Is the tracksuit a sleight of hand that does both at the same time?

AKINGBADE   I guess the popularity of sportswear is to do with the rise of grime music and people appealing to that, although they have no relation to it. It's just cool. It reminds me of how in university my class was full of people who had family houses in the countryside but they wore tattered clothes most of the time — the worst clothes ever. I did not understand that. Why would they do that? But I think for them it was the opposite idea: they had something to hide, and they wanted to make sure that people didn't learn too much about them.

WEBB   Why is it that certain people might want to hide class privilege?

SPERLING: There's maybe two aspects to this. On the one hand, there's a kind of obfuscation about material circumstances which has to be a tactic for maintaining class advantage, even if unconsciously. That's something that I write about a little bit in my novel: one of the catalysts for the plot is the main character's dawning awareness in his late twenties of how some of the people in his circle, who seemed to be living the same sort of life as him, are now buying flats and houses with money from their parents, they'd had that resource of inherited wealth all along but never mentioned it. On the other hand there's the way that these anxieties about class play out in people's performance of their social identities. Which can often be as ridiculous, or funny, or touching, as it is sinister. Of course, the idea that some identities are more authentic or more real than others is a totally sentimental, stupid one. But it does seem to be persistent.

FASHION PLACES

WEBB   Ray and Ayo, you both grew up in Hackney in East London. It's an incredibly complicated area in terms of how it's changed over the years, having recently seen an influx of wealthier, largely white professionals and creatives. How have you registered that change?
AKINGBADE   I first noticed it in 2008, when I was in secondary school. I participated in a photography competition and we shot photos around Dalston. There were these specific types of trendy white people going down Kingsland High Street, and I remember asking the teacher, 'Are there fashion places near here?' I was so confused because I didn't associate Dalston with high fashion glam. I still have the photos I took that day.

There are certain areas my friends and I don't go to. I don't like Broadway Market, even though I practically live on its doorstep, the strip makes me feel uncomfortable. But at the same time, I had a conversation with another friend who said, 'Change happens. You have to accept that.' I definitely accept it, but I don't feel like if I do go down there I'm respected, in a sense. Because I am looked upon as the Other, and I think there's a lack of compassion there. I just feel like it's not for me. So it's bittersweet. Hackney is my hometown but I'm just edging to get away from it.
ANTROBUS   Yes, I feel you, and there's loads I want to say to that. Did you notice in London Fields, right next to Broadway Market, when we were growing up, did they have lamp posts, lights at night?
AKINGBADE   No.
ANTROBUS   No, it was all dark.
AKINGBADE   There were lots of gangs there, stabbings. You did not walk down that way.
ANTROBUS   No one walked down there or drove down there. Then, like you said, from 2008, as soon as the change started happening, that's one of the first things they did. They lit all the paths in the park. That to me was insulting, like now people finally care about the lives out here.
WEBB   Ayo, I'm reminded of your film *Tower XYZ*, where the narrator repeats that phrase 'Let's get rid of the ghetto, let's get rid of the ghetto.'
AKINGBADE   My role there is like an archivist, researching and documenting what is perceived as history.
WEBB   Do you think a filmmaker or artist needs to be part of the community they're trying to

archive to archive it successfully, or meaningfully?
AKINGBADE   I don't believe in artists making art about subjects and not being involved in their community. There's a lot of that going on in the creative industry, especially among new-media video artists. It begs the question of whether you are making art for the institution or for the actual community you're trying to make money off.

WHOSE CULTURAL CAPITAL?

DENMAN-CLEAVER   The other thing happening here is the demolition or handing over of public spaces to different communities. The Jobcentre isn't a Jobcentre anymore because the council have decided not to provide that service. The Working Men's clubs were to do with workers' rights and unions, and we don't have those anymore. They're all being dismantled, so working men's clubs are available for sale, to be occupied by whoever can afford to drink there. I think it's really important to acknowledge the infrastructures that are put in place for white working-, middle- or upper-middle-class communities, and the spaces that are sold off, housing estates, or the flats that are possibly rentable but not affordably buyable. I think that underpins some of these more individualistic fashion decisions.
WEBB   In the food chain of gentrification, where's the tipping point between who is responsible? Usually there's an area of the city which is affordable to live in by the terms of middle-class, usually white artists or creatives who then come into the area and populate it with 'cultural capital', in air quotes because it's white middle-class cultural capital. That shoots up the prices because more people are coming in and the whole fabric of the area changes. But if we agree that artists need to produce art, they need to live somewhere they can afford to live — how do we make good with that balance?
ANTROBUS   I want to introduce an example of positive gentrification I've seen in Hackney. There was a little bike shop set up six, seven years ago, and everyone that worked there built bikes. Some of them were also graphic designers and artists, but they happened to share the skill of knowing how to make bikes. So they set up a bike shop in the middle of this estate near where I live and every Saturday they had a board saying 'Free cycle workshops'. They taught specifically refugees, unemployed people and people on benefits. You

just had to show up as a member of this community and engage. This project ran for about two years, and every time I saw it I thought, 'This is beautiful', because they were creating a meaningful engagement with the people who were already there. That's ultimately what it's about for me, you need to be engaging with the people who already exist there, as opposed to creating these Jobcentre bars which are a way to acknowledge it but not really acknowledge it. That's the insult of it.

DENMAN-CLEAVER   Something I've been thinking about a lot is that in Newcastle the council allowed artists to have hundreds of studios in the city centre, and now they've created the cultural capital that was desired they've chucked the artists out and replaced the studios with retail units. I think it's not necessarily about the individual artists, but it's about knowing how you might be instrumentalised. You're always complicit in it, but it's about knowing to what extent you're being used, what your threshold is, what you're prepared to do to create that bike shop.

POSTCODE LOTTERY

WEBB   The 2017 State of the Nation Report for the Social Mobility Commission revealed a 'stark mobility postcode lottery' in Britain. The chair of the commission said, 'The country seems to be in an ever growing spiral of reinforcing division' and that 'London and its hinterland are increasingly looking like a different country from the rest of Britain, accounting for two thirds of all social mobility hotspots.' How is that ever going to change? How do you see that changing, who belongs in London?

DENMAN-CLEAVER   The Arts Council have changed the percentage of funding they give to London, and there have been a lot of major cuts to funding in London as opposed to the rest of the country. I think moving their offices to Manchester is kind of a symbolic thing that goes along with that, but they have changed. Actually, in my personal experience of talking to people in the arts, it's much easier to get funding outside of London because there's fewer people applying.

AKINGBADE   But then it makes everything even more competitive in London! BFI Network now split their funds across networks in Manchester and Sussex, too. And London Calling, a major London film fund, has either stopped or changed its remit.

DENMAN-CLEAVER   People in the North sometimes call the move to London 'brain drain'. There's a version of success which is connected to London or moving away, moving to the big city. But maybe in the long term there'll be a shift where that's not necessary, because Sheffield and Liverpool have their own creative centres and cultural identities, and they are really busy because people can afford to do stuff there. Maybe that will change rather than becoming hyper-competitive.

NARRATIVES OF SUCCESS

WEBB   There is this narrative, growing up anywhere outside of London, that you can go to London and try and find success there.

DENMAN-CLEAVER   It goes back to your point, Ray, about defining your own version of success.

ANTROBUS   Yeah, you have to get specific so that you know what you're taking responsibility for, and then you're empowered by that. You used the word 'narrative' there, Ralf, that's a pure capitalistic narrative as opposed to a personal one. For example, when I was younger and spending time in Jamaica there was a big question about whether I was going to go to school there. I had a few cousins who'd moved back from the States and London and started going to school in Kingston. And every one of them had to re-do two years of education to catch up. Here they were good students, but in Jamaica they were so far behind everyone else. People assume that the best education you can get might be in London or Cambridge or Oxford, but these are capitalistic narratives.

WEBB   Do we – culturally, politically – talk about social mobility as though it's a good in-and-of itself?

SPERLING: I suppose the danger of focusing on social mobility is that it legitimises higher levels of inequality. Every story about the market-stall trader who ends up as a billionaire makes it seem more acceptable that the boss of a company can earn a hundred times more than his lowest employee. It's that New Labour thing: you can be intensely relaxed about some people getting filthy rich if you can cling on to the idea that anyone could be one of those people. But as you say, all the studies suggest that social mobility is pretty limited anyway, especially in the UK, and people's outcomes are pretty closely related to their family background. So yeah, maybe we need to talk more about reducing inequality than about increasing social mobility. You need to compress the range, so that people in the lower classes earn a higher minimum wage, have stronger collective bargaining, maybe have a universal basic income, that sort of thing, and can live in conditions of material comfort and dignity. This is all boring sort of policy stuff to do with redistribution and interventions in the labour market and that sort of thing, but I think there are some suggestions that a shift in this direction is slowly happening. That we've reached what Danny Dorling calls 'peak inequality' and there's now a broad appetite for a shift to the left in policy terms. If we lived in a less unequal society then the question of social mobility would be less vexed, and less important.

'IT'S GRIM UP NORTH'

WEBB   Talking more broadly about the London-regional divide, how have you experienced this in the wake of Brexit? After the vote I encountered an attitude of anti-regionalism from London friends, who decided that everyone in the rest of the country must be racist and uneducated.

DENMAN-CLEAVER   I have an example a colleague told me relating to that, which links back to what we were talking about in terms of compassion and how we understand the relationship between class and racism, and the structures that do or don't support compassion. In an area of Newcastle that's historically really deprived, very white and very cut off from the rest of the city, known as a place where there's loads of racial tension and aggression, there are these huge blocks of houses that were condemned as uninhabitable by humans, so all the traditionally white working-class or not-working communities were kicked out. But then the quota for taking refugee and migrant communities increased, so without doing anything to the buildings, very literally in the middle of the night, people arrived in buses and refugees were housed in these blocks of flats that had been deemed uninhabitable.

We need to better understand the situations in which people encounter migration or asylum-seeking communities, and how circumstance might breed racism on a societal level. There's the presumption that everyone voted Brexit because they're racists. Well, actually, the way that race plays out in those poorer communities is often unsupported and violently imposed by local authorities.

SPERLING   It seems to me that a lot of the Brexit debate is constructed out of political elites' projections about what they want the North to stand for. But that has real effects. You get an episode of *Question Time* where the producers have gone and found all these gammon-faced guys to sit in the audience and ask objectionable questions. One thing I find really depressing at the moment is this constant debate in the Labour party: do we need to be a bit more anti-immigration to appeal to some idea of authenticity in the heartland? I feel that's just a fantasy of Westminster journalists and politicians who are building up these ideas of what the people are like there.

DENMAN-CLEAVER   Which isn't that far away from that completely generalised idea of what people are like outside of London. The 'it's grim up north' thing.

ANGER

WEBB   A year or so after living in London and being in the literary world, I got very very angry and very resentful of the amount of wealth there was in the industry, the social connections people had, and the lack of recognition of those things. But also at the same time I had to acknowledge that I hadn't had a particularly difficult struggle to get to where I was. I realised that what annoys me the most is when people don't acknowledge their class privilege.

DENMAN-CLEAVER   You can't have compassion for different class situations if you actually do not understand them. When I've gone into local authority offices to contest decisions, the individuals with power have no tangible everyday notion of what it would mean to actually need a library; that you cannot get a job if you don't have a computer in a library to use. I don't know how you breed compassion when there is a total lack of knowledge.

ANTROBUS   We've been talking a lot about compassion but we also need compassion for ourselves. I recognise that anger and frustration but I also think it's important to model that compassion, as once you embody it, you become an example of it.

DENMAN-CLEAVER   Do you think that's also about trying to find a way to be more comfortable with the class betrayal thing? It's okay to have wanted that and to have got it.

AKINGBADE   The social climbing question.

The common aspiration to move up equates to success. You get rid of your old friends, move away from your council estate, and hope for that eureka moment when all your problems will be solved. But history has taught us that does not mean much if you are not strong within yourself, because imposter syndrome might come to play. Being a black person, I think cultural hybridity will always come to play: I was born in the UK, but my family are from Nigeria, so I experience a plethora of different traditions and customs at once. It's multifaceted, not easy to define. Stuart Hall wrote extensively about this.

'GET OUT OF THE WAY'

SPERLING   It's also the question of what to do in the situation when you realise social mobility and forming networks is easier to do as a white person. Would the ethical thing to do be to step back? In my day job I work for a university, and rising up and getting graduate opportunities is partly about building networks and getting more senior people to treat you as a peer. It is all totally class and race coded. Straight down the line. So in that sense I'm in a position where I'm a beneficiary of a system of exclusion.

DENMAN-CLEAVER   More and more I keep seeing examples of well-intentioned — and this goes back to our discussion about inclusivity — projects or exhibitions, but where the person who made it happen through certain privilege, be it class or race or sexuality or whatever, just won't get out of the fucking way. They still want it to be seen as, 'I allowed these people to do this'. As for inclusivity, I'm probably okay with quotas but I think the next step is to make sure it doesn't loop back to: 'We did this because a lot of people weren't here, but now you're here so we're okay.' Instead it needs to be: 'You need to have this space and it's yours and we need to be accountable to you, not to ourselves and our own decisions.' I think that until people get out of the way and hand it over, things aren't going to change.

WISTERIA

OLGA TOKARCZUK
tr. ANTONIA LLOYD-JONES

From downstairs I could hear their every step. Ever since she'd married that was my main occupation – listening in on them, following their movements, counting their steps and building ingenious images to fit them. From kitchen to living room, then bathroom, back to the kitchen, then the living room again, the bedroom, the creak of the large bed left by my mother, thus her grandmother, two metres wide, its mattress still springy. Of course I could tell her footsteps (faster and lighter) from his (sometimes he glided as if the slippers she'd bought him were too big). The footsteps would come together and move apart, meet and pass each other by. I would close the windows to hear them better, for even the distant jingle of trams disturbed me – there's a depot quite near here. We live on the outskirts in an old, well-kept residential district amid pre-war houses covered in creepers, just like this one. A cool stairwell, a ground floor and a first floor. I'm on the ground floor, I let them have the first floor.

There's a huge wisteria growing by the front steps – it's a beautiful plant, but it's dissolute too. Every summer it blooms, and its elongated clusters of flowers dangle like nipples. Each shoot grows a metre per year, so one has to remember not to leave the windows and balcony doors open in summer – otherwise the shoots push their way into the house, seek out the larger holes in the restless texture of the net curtains, and it looks as if they're trying to reach the furniture, sit on the chairs at the table... Ah, I'd serve that plant tea in my best cups, I'd treat it to rich Turkish pastries.

But in fact I sat down to tea alone, shifted my gaze to the ceiling, and then by following their footsteps I'd recreate every moment of their life. It was tame and monotonous. My daughter was incapable of providing him with entertainment. Whenever silence reigned up there for a long time, whenever there was no movement, it meant they were watching television – they were sitting on the sofa. His hand on her arm, thigh by thigh, a glass of beer on the side table, orange juice next to her, the newspaper open at the television guide. She was sure to be filing her nails (she'd always been obsessed with them), and he'd be reading. Silence in the kitchen meant they were eating. At most the shuffle of a chair moving back when one of them got up to fetch the salt. The roar of water in the bathroom meant one of them was washing. I learned to recognise which – she spent less time bathing, whereas he stood under the shower for far longer than seemed necessary. What could he be doing there, fragile and soluble under a stream of hot water, like smooth soap? Scrubbing his back? Washing his hair? Motionlessly contemplating the trails of water trickling down his naked body? Then came silence, the roar of water would stop, he'd probably be standing in front of the mirror to shave. I learned to see this precisely – he'd smear shaving cream on his beautiful face, then carefully remove it with a razor blade, until his skin appeared smooth and fresh. With a towel around his hips, barefoot, with droplets of water on his back, he was renewable. Then I'd imagine briefly cuddling up to him from behind, I'd imagine I was incorporeal, that I could feel him, but he couldn't feel me. He was innocent, and I reached for his hips. But then, after his shave, she always came and tenderly smeared cream on him, she must have aroused him while doing it, thrusting her hand beneath his towel, and from there the footsteps led into the bedroom and imperceptibly changed into the gentle wheeze of the old bedsprings. After all, they were a married couple. It's normal, I told myself. I'd go out into the garden. I'd pull on a pair of rubber gloves and weed the flowerbeds. I'd make holes in the earth with a finger and spit in them. I'd fondle the thick, sinewy roots of dahlias. My head would start to spin when I straightened up too suddenly.

My daughter – a beautiful young woman with a slightly eastern look and long, straight, jet-black hair (from her father). My daughter is 26, but I know it's just an illusion. In reality she's younger – I witnessed the moment she stopped maturing at the age of 17, one night, one day she reached her peak and then glided into the future along a sort of plateau, as if she were on skates. And she's still 17 – she'll die as a 17-year-old.

As soon as she found out she was pregnant, she came to me here downstairs, with her belly exposed according to the latest fashion, she pouted, stood in the typical pose of a pregnant woman with her hands resting on her hips and said: 'I don't feel well.' I made her some tea or chamomile. She also said: 'Oleg is so worried about me, he loves me so much.' But she miscarried. He took her to the hospital, came back, spent ages on the phone, then jangled bottles on the stairs and that evening he drank beer while watching television. I brought him supper, I stirred his tea with my finger, and then I licked that finger. I put him to bed on the sofa. He looked at me from below, from afar. I only loosened his leather belt; he mumbled 'thank you' and fell asleep. That night I poked around in their flat. I inspected the underwear neatly piled in the cupboard, the toiletries in the bathroom, the streaks of fingers on the mirror, the single hairs in the bath tub, a heap of dirty clothes in a wicker basket, and the black leather wallet that gently fitted the shape of his buttocks.

My body was obstructing me, my body was tiresome, for I'd have been happy to lie down beside him incorporeally. This body of mine swelled as we passed each other on the stairs. He spoke to me from a distance that was too short, too dangerous, for it was full of scents. The jumpsuit woven from scented air crackled like a zip fastener being opened, and every possible gesture was acted out around it – innocent ones, pats on the back full of solace, as well as his hand between my legs. I told him to close the windows at night to keep out the wisteria, to empty the postbox regularly, to do this and that.

I'd desired him from the moment I saw him. Is that a bad thing? After all, daughters are part of their mothers, just as mothers are part of their daughters – no wonder desire goes roaring through them both like a river in flood, no wonder it fills all possible spaces located lower down. I am a certain age and I know one cannot fight against a craving – one needs to be a sensitive enricher of the soil – let it flow, let it drift, for it can't be either satisfied or stopped. Anyone who thinks otherwise is fooling themselves. He thought otherwise.

But first she returned and in my kitchen we danced that sad dance of ours – we swayed in each other's arms, stepping from foot to foot in a repetitious ballet all around the kitchen, from window to door, a single person again, from before the wrongful divide. We stroked each other's hair, immersed in each other's scent, sank into my collars and her hoods. I could feel her breasts and her empty belly. But when he appeared in the doorway, we moved away from each other in embarrassment; he took her away, and then I heard their footsteps upstairs again.

I taught her how to dig out the roots of perennials and how to cover the quilt in a single move. At night he would come to me downstairs and he must have been afraid of me, because he always smelled of beer. I would wrap my legs around his hips as if I were a young girl. Next morning I'd hear his shower – even longer, even more motionless than before.

He probably thought in his own way, that any desire can be assuaged, any thirst quenched, any hunger satisfied – just like a man.

We closed the windows for the winter; once again we had to prune the shoots of the climber with a knife. It still rapped its stumps against the window panes to the beat of the first autumn winds, but it hadn't a chance; it gazed at us from the window ledges, leafless and helpless now. The heaters made the air quiver.

Did she, my daughter, know? If she was part of me, just as I was part of her, she must have known the truth. Sometimes I heard her wake up in the night and cry out: 'Mama!', but it wasn't a summons, I didn't have to leap from my bed and run to her any more. She cried 'Mama!' but she could just as well have cried 'Aah!' or 'Ooh!' He was the one who hugged her. He was the one who said 'It's all right now, go to sleep.'

Winter was gradually advancing, tenaciously making the world darker. Plaintive long nights, short days crumbled into the sound of footsteps upstairs. She didn't speak to me, so I said nothing either. Whenever she left the house I'd watch the back of her head through the window. And whenever I left the house I'd sense her gaze on mine. I'd see her as if casually making holes in the earth with her umbrella as she walked to the stop, and spitting into them. I'd hear the sharp flick of a freshly covered quilt.

Many times in her absence I treated him to coffee. I'd sprinkle two spoonfuls of sugar into the glass and stir it long enough for the sweetness to soothe the bitterness. He drank it avidly, without looking up, he drank to the dregs. I always made the first subtle move, almost imperceptible, and not because mine was the greater desire, but to free him from a sense of guilt, to allow him the comfort of being a victim, to absolve him before the sin had been committed. I'd fling my legs onto his hips and restrain that boundless urge of his. I didn't want him to be weak, I wanted him to be strong.

Then she would come home and make him her own coffee. She'd sweeten it with two spoonfuls of sugar and stir it long enough for the drink to be like velvet.

So it went on until spring, when the constancy of a well-balanced structure became impossible to bear. That same day, in her coffee and in mine, the second spoonful didn't sprinkle sugar. As it happened on the same day, it was clear to both of us that daughters are part of their mothers and mothers are part of their daughters. There could be no other explanation. And so he died twice over. He was twice deceased. Once for her and once for me.

She ran down the stairs barefoot and we threw our arms around each other, weeping and sobbing. We began to sway, one step, two, hugging each other, in pyjamas and night shirt. All she kept whispering was, 'He died, he died!', while I kept saying, 'He's dead, he's dead'.

Yet we knew something that he did not, neither while he was still alive, nor now that he was dead – that life after death is just the same kind of dream as life before death. That death is really an illusion, and it's not at all hard to go on playing. And I was the one who started it, quite automatically, as if I'd always known this difficult ritual, and she just copied me. She soon realised what it was about, and now we were both whispering to the ceiling for him to come back. I did wonder why we were looking up, because death is neither up nor down, neither above nor below, nor is it left or right, inside or outside. So I was telling us to get it right, to accept the general rules, to address death where it was, in other words everywhere. By now we were banging our fists on the walls and floor, shouting instead of whispering. I focused to make sure our words would reach him, to make sure he'd understand their meaning. I was sure as well that just like others, he thought dying meant simply ceasing to exist. 'Oleg,' I kept repeating slowly and clearly, 'Oleg, the situation is far more complicated.' How do you persuade someone who isn't there to take courage and start to exist again? And as for that beautiful daughter of mine with the eastern looks, she fully understood this bizarre, strangely metaphysical problem – that anything is possible, that the rhizomes of reality tauten in our heads, ready to grow. All that is there is what one believes is there. There are no other rules. So we banged our fists on the walls of the house like furies, shouting and calling. As if to a child she cried over and over, appealing to his common sense, 'Stop it now, wake up, it's not true that you've died, just think about it logically.' And I was saying, 'Oleg, I beg you, look at it from another angle, just make one small effort.'

And finally he appeared. His outline was still slightly blurred, as if he'd jumped out of a television screen. His figure was quivering. He was angry and confused. I saw him first – after all, I am of a certain age. She saw him a little later. And at once I touched him to see if he'd forgotten about his body, about his desire. But everything was in order. The outline settled, the flickering stopped. And then, as if collecting my reward, I laid him on the floor and kissed him hard on the mouth; he passionately returned that kiss. His lips materialised under mine. Then she took the next step, and now he was clearly alive.

It was just the right time to open the windows and lure the tender new shoots of wisteria into the dark inside.

AYO AKINGBADE is an artist and filmmaker. Born in Hackney, she studied film at the London College of Communication, and lives and works in London. She produced, directed and edited the short film *Tower XYZ* (2016), which received a Special Mention Award at the International Short Film Festival Oberhausen and won the inaugural Sonja Savić Award at the Alternative Film/ Video Festival, Belgrade. She is a recipient of the Sundance Institute Ignite Fellowship (2018) for emerging filmmakers and has been selected for Bloomberg New Contemporaries (2018). *Street 66* (2018) is about Brixtonite housing activist Theodora Boatemah MBE and her influence on the regeneration of Angell Town Estate in Brixton. It premiered at International Film Festival Rotterdam and screened at the Institute of Contemporary Arts in London and Sheffield Doc/Fest.

RAYMOND ANTROBUS was born in Hackney to an English mother and Jamaican father. He is the author of *To Sweeten Bitter* and *The Perseverance*, which has just been selected as the Poetry Book Society's 2018 Winter Choice. He is a founding member of Chill Pill and Keats House Poets Forum, and the recipient of fellowships from Cave Canem, Complete Works 3 and Jerwood Compton Poetry. He is also one of the world's first recipients of an MA in Spoken Word education from Goldsmiths University. In 2018 he was awarded The Geoffrey Dearmer Prize.

NANAE AOYAMA was born in 1983 in Saitama, and currently lives in Tokyo. In 2005, she won the Bungei Prize with her short story 'Mado no Akari' (The Light of Windows), written while she was at university. Her short story collection *Hitori Biyori* (A Perfect Day to Be Alone) was awarded the 136th Akutagawa Prize in 2007, and in 2009, her story 'Fragments' was awarded the 35th Yasunari Kawabata Literary Award, making her the award's youngest ever recipient. Her work has been translated into various languages, including Chinese, German, Italian, and French.

JULIA ARMFIELD was born in London in 1990. She is a fiction writer and occasional playwright with a Masters in Victorian Art and Literature from Royal Holloway University. Her work has been published in *Lighthouse*, *Analog Magazine*, *Neon Magazine* and *The Stockholm Review*. She was

commended in the Moth Short Story Prize 2017 and longlisted for the Deborah Rogers Award 2018. Her first book, *salt slow*, will be published by Picador in 2019. 'The Great Awake' is the winner of the White Review Short Story Prize 2018.

POLLY BARTON is a translator of Japanese literature and non-fiction, currently based in Bristol. Other authors she has translated include Aoko Matsuda, Naocola Yamazaki and Misumi Kubo. Her translation of *Spring Garden* by Tomoka Shibasaki is out from Pushkin Press.

A. K. BLAKEMORE is the author of *Humbert Summer* (Eyewear, 2015) and *Fondue* (Offord Road Books, 2018). Her work has been widely published and anthologised, appearing in journals and magazines including *Poetry*, *The London Review of Books*, *Poetry Review* and *Poetry London*.

KEVIN BRAZIL teaches English at the University of Southampton, and lives in London. He is the author of *Art, History, and Postwar Fiction*, forthcoming from Oxford University Press.

IMOGEN CASSELS's poems have appeared in the *London Review of Books*, *Blackbox Manifold*, *Cumulus*, *Datableed*, *Ambit*, and on the London Underground. She is a first-year PhD student at Cambridge.

ZINZI CLEMMONS was raised in Philadelphia by a South African mother and an American father. Her debut novel, *What We Lose* (Viking 2017) was a finalist for the Aspen Words Literary Prize, a Hurston/Wright Legacy Award, and the National Book Critics Circle Leonard Prize. She is a 2017 National Book Award 5 Under 35 Honoree. She wrote the foreword for a new edition of Jean Toomer's *Cane*, forthcoming from Penguin Classics in 2019. She is a professor of English at Occidental College in Los Angeles.

TESS DENMAN-CLEAVER is a North East-based artist whose work spans live performance, performance writing, artist publication and performative workshops. She has a PhD in performance philosophy and landscape. Her recent work has been presented at Hatton Gallery (Newcastle), Tyneside Cinema (Newcastle), Workplace Gallery (Gateshead), Tate St Ives and Turner Contemporary (Margate).

LAUREN ELKIN is a writer and translator. Most recently the author of *Flâneuse: Women Walk the City* (Chatto & Windus/FSG), which was shortlisted for the PEN/Diamondstein-Spielvogel Prize for the Art of the Essay and was a *New York Times* Notable book of 2017 as well as a Radio 4 Book of the Week, she is currently at work on her next book, *Art Monsters*. She lives in Paris.

REBECCA GOSS is the author of two full-length poetry collections, *The Anatomy of Structures* (Flambard, 2010) and *Her Birth* (Carcanet/ Northern House, 2013). In 2014, she was selected for The Poetry Book Society's Next Generation Poets. Her collaboration with the photographer Chris Routledge will be published in 2018 with Guillemot Press. Carcanet will publish her third full-length collection, *Girl*, in 2019. She is Creative Writing Fellow at Liverpool John Moores University.

ALLISON KATZ is an artist, currently based in London. Forthcoming solo exhibitions in the autumn of 2018 will open at Gió Marconi, Milan and Antenna Space, Shanghai. Her first monograph will be published in early 2019 by JRP-Ringier.

SANDIP KURIAKOSE graduated with an MVA (Painting) from MS University, Baroda and a BFA (Painting) from the College of Art, New Delhi. His shows include FotoFest International 2018 Biennial Central Exhibition INDIA — Contemporary Photographic and New Media Art, Houston; Regimes of Truth, Gati Dance Forum, New Delhi; Against the Order Of, Clark House Initiative, Mumbai; The 6th European Month of Photography, Das Foto Image Factory, Berlin; Art For Young Collectors, Galerie Mirchandani + Steinruecke, Mumbai; and United Art Fair, New Delhi, among others. His residencies include Clark House Initiative (2018), CONA Foundation (2018), TIFA Working Studios (2018) and the Summer Residency Program, School of Visual Arts (2013). He lives and works in New Delhi.

ANTONIA LLOYD-JONES has translated works by several of Poland's leading contemporary novelists and reportage authors, as well as crime fiction, poetry and children's books, and is the 2018 winner of the Transatlantyk Award for the most outstanding promoter of Polish literature abroad. She is a mentor for the Emerging Translators' Mentorship Programme, and a former co-chair of the UK Translators Association.

LINA MERUANE is an award-winning Chilean writer and scholar, teaching at New York University. She is the author of five novels; *Sangre en el ojo*, her most recent, received the prestigious Sor Juana Inés de la Cruz Novel Prize in Mexico and has been translated into English (*Seeing Red*, Atlantic) and several other languages. Among her non-fiction books are *Viral Voyages* (Palgrave Macmillan) and her essayistic memoir *Volverse Palestina*, to which the piece published here is a follow-up.

EVAN MOFFITT is a writer and critic based in New York. He is the associate editor of *frieze*.

ANDREA ROSENBERG is a translator from the Spanish and Portuguese. Among her recent and forthcoming full-length translations are Tomás González's *The Storm* (Archipelago Books, 2018), Inês Pedrosa's *In Your Hands* (AmazonCrossing, 2018), Aura Xilonen's *The Gringo Champion* (Europa Editions, 2016), Juan Gómez Bárcena's *The Sky over Lima* (Houghton Mifflin Harcourt, 2016), and David Jiménez's *Children of the Monsoon* (Autumn Hill Books, 2014).

BETTINA SAMSON (b. 1978) is a French artist whose protean work delves into science and the history of modernity, mixing documentary reference and individual narratives. Drawing from craft techniques and materials, her practice gives way to unexpected and improvised forms.

MATTHEW SPERLING's first novel, *Astroturf*, was published by riverrun in August. He is a lecturer in English Literature at UCL.

OLGA TOKARCZUK is one of Poland's best and most beloved authors. Her novel *Flights* won the 2018 Man Booker International Prize, in Jennifer Croft's translation. In 2015 she received the Brueckepreis and the prestigious annual literary award from Poland's Ministry of Culture and National Heritage, as well as — for the second time — Poland's highest literary honour, the Nike and the Nike Readers' Prize for *Books of Jacob*. She is the author of nine novels and three short story collections, and her work has been translated into a dozen languages.

PLATES

Cover	Allison Katz, *AK WR 23*, 2018
I	Allison Katz, *Le Tit*, 2010. 28 × 43.2 cm, ed. 150 + 10.
II	Allison Katz, *The Parts (Menagerie [The Century])*, 2011. 45.7 × 61 cm, ed. 2 + 1.
III	Allison Katz, *fig-futures (Split)*, 2018. 84.1 × 118.9 cm, ed. 10 + 2.
IV	Allison Katz and Camilla Wills, *Perra Perdida (Found in Quebec)*, 2013. 40 × 56 cm, ed. 20 + 5.
V	Allison Katz, *Shelf Painting Poster 3*, 2016. 54 × 90 cm, ed. 5 + 1.
VI	Allison Katz, *Daymark (Opening)*, 2012. 65 × 87 cm, ed 10 + 2.
VII	Allison Katz, *AKgraph*, 2013. 84.1 × 118.9 cm, ed. 25 + 5.
VIII	Allison Katz, *Last seen entering the Biltmore*, 2014. 72.5 × 102.6 cm, ed. 10 + 2.
IX	Allison Katz, *Antenna Space at Paris Internationale (Caveman)*, 2017. 59.4 × 84.1 cm, ed. 10 + 2.
X	Allison Katz, *fig-2 week 47/50*, 2015. 42 × 60 cm, ed. 300 + 25.
XI	Allison Katz, *Rumours, Echoes (Alfama)*, 2014. 42 × 60 cm, ed. 10 + 2.
XII	Allison Katz, *The Song Cave Press Edition No. 6*, 2014. 43.2 × 61 cm, ed. 50 + 5.
XIII	Allison Katz, *Diary w/o Dates (Mum as Nippy)*, 2018. 38.8 × 59.4 cm.
XIV	Allison Katz, *Diary w/o Dates (Adult Services)*, 2018. 84.1 × 118.9 cm, ed. 15 + 2.
XV	Allison Katz, *We boil at different degrees*, 2016. 84.1 × 59.4 cm, ed. 500 + 100.
XVI – XXVI	Courtesy the artist and Galerie Sultana.
XVI	Bettina Samson, *Kink (More Honor'd in the Breach) I*, 2015, Terracotta, 37 × 28 × 31 cm.
XVII	Bettina Samson, *Kink (More Honor'd in the Breach) II*, 2015, Terracotta, 25 × 53 × 34 cm.
XVIII	Bettina Samson, *Kink (More Honor'd in the Breach) III*, 2015, Terracotta, 45 × 30 × 30 cm.
XIX	Bettina Samson, *Kink (More Honor'd in the Breach) IV*, 2015, Terracotta, 45 × 41 × 33 cm.
XX	Bettina Samson, *Mètis & Metiista I*, 2013, borosilicate glass, 17 × 28 × 17 cm.
XXI	Bettina Samson, *Mètis & Metiista II*, 2013, borosilicate glass, 41, 5 × 31 × 16 cm.
XXII	Bettina Samson, *Mètis & Metiista V*, 2013, borosilicate glass, 42 × 22 × 22 cm.
XXIII	Bettina Samson, *Mètis & Metiista II*, 2013, borosilicate glass, 22 × 33 × 9 cm.
XXIV	Bettina Samson, *L'éclat 9*, 2011, enameled ceramic and platinum sheen, 34 × 7 × 7 cm.
XXV	Bettina Samson, *L'éclat 6*, 2011, enameled ceramic and platinum sheen, 10 × 8 × 7 cm.
XXVI	Bettina Samson, *L'éclat 12*, 2011, enameled ceramic and platinum sheen, 36 × 13 × 8 cm.
p. 124	Mernet Larsen, *Shoppers*, 1987. Acrylic on canvas, 49 × 66 in., courtesy the artist and James Cohan, New York.
p. 125	Mernet Larsen, *Shoppers*, 1987, acrylic, oil, tracing paper on canvas, 54 × 54 in., courtesy the artist and James Cohan, New York.
p. 126	Nicolas Poussin, *Landscape with a Man Washing his Feet at a Fountain*, c. 1648.
p. 127	Mernet Larsen, *Landscape with a Dirt Road (from Poussin)*, 2011, acrylic and tracing paper on canvas, 26 × 54 in., courtesy the artist and James Cohan, New York.
p. 128	Mernet Larsen, *Explanation*, 2007, acrylic and tracing paper on canvas, 41 × 52 in., courtesy the artist and James Cohan, New York.
p. 129	Mernet Larsen, *Chainsawer and Bicyclist*, 2014, acrylic and mixed media on canvas, 49 1/2 × 49 in., courtesy the artist and James Cohan, New York.
p. 130	Mernet Larsen, *Untitled photograph of the artist's father*, 1960, black and white photograph, 5 × 7 in., courtesy the artist and James Cohan, New York.
XXVII – XXXIII	Paintings from Mernet Larsen's recent exhibition *Situation Rooms*, James Cohan, New York, April 19 – June 16, 2018.
XXVII	Mernet Larsen, *Drawing Hands*, 2017, acrylic and mixed media on canvas, 67 1/2 × 36 1/4 in.
XXVIII	Mernet Larsen, *Cabinet Meeting (with Coffee)*, 2018, acrylic and mixed media on canvas, 52 1/2 × 50 in.
XXIX	Mernet Larsen, *Cabinet Meeting*, 2017, acrylic and mixed media on canvas, 61 × 65 1/4 in.
XXX	Mernet Larsen, *Cup Tricks*, 2018, acrylic and mixed media on canvas, 57 × 38 1/4 in.
XXXI	Mernet Larsen, *Hand Slap Game*, 2018, acrylic and mixed media on canvas, 67 3/4 × 20 1/2 in.
XXXII	Mernet Larsen, *Situation Room (Scissors, Rocks, Paper)*, 2018, acrylic and mixed media on canvas, 62 1/2 × 51 1/2 in.
XXXIII	Mernet Larsen, *Lecture*, 2011. Acrylic and mixed media on canvas, 58 × 36 in.
XXXIV – XXXIX	Studies - in correspondence with Mernet Larsen's recent exhibition *Situation Rooms*, James Cohan, New York, April 19 - June 16, 2018.
XXXIV	Mernet Larsen, *Board*, 2017. Acrylic on Bristol paper, 24 × 19 in.

XXXV   Mernet Larsen, *Cabinet Meeting: Study*, 2017. Acrylic on Bristol paper, 19 × 24 in.
XXXVI   Mernet Larsen, *Situation Room: Explanation*, 2017. Acrylic on Bristol paper, 19 × 24 in.
XXXVII   Mernet Larsen, *Situation Room: Scissors/Rock/Paper*, 2017. Acrylic on Bristol paper, 19 × 24 in.
XXXVIII   Mernet Larsen, *Cabinet #2*, 2017. Acrylic on Bristol paper, 24 × 19 in.
XXXIX   Mernet Larsen, *Situation Room: Oblique*, 2017. Acrylic on Bristol paper, 19 × 24 in.

*Drive Your Plow Over the Bones
of the Dead* by Olga Tokarczuk
(tr. Antonia Lloyd-Jones) is
published by Fitzcarraldo Editions
on 12 September 2018.

'Suffused with William Blake,
astrological lore, and the landscapes
of middle Europe, Tokarczuk's latest
novel is both a meditation on human
compassion and a murder mystery
that lingers in the imagination.'
— Marcel Theroux, author
of *Strange Bodies*

Fitzcarraldo Editions

DAS HUND

FOR

FREEDOM

DEBUT
ALBUM
OUT NOW

DAS HUND – FOR FREEDOM TOUR

© FRENCH RIVIERA RECO

15 SEPTEMBER, FRENCH RIVIERA, LONDON
22 SEPTEMBER, LIMBO, MARGATE FESTIVAL
02 OCTOBER, DRAF X KOKO, LONDON
11 OCTOBER, EXETER PHOENIX, EXETER
31 OCTOBER, THE TETLEY, LEEDS
03 NOVEMBER, TŶ PAWB, WREXHAM
08 NOVEMBER, g39, CARDIFF
15 NOVEMBER, KARST, PLYMOUTH
24/25 NOVEMBER, MACKINTOSH LANE, LONDON

frenchriviera1988.com

Supported using public fund
ARTS COUN
ENGLAND
LOTTERY FUNDED

Laura Langer

22 September to 21 October

Matthew Richardson

3 November to 9 December

Piper Keys
Exhibitions

Supported using public funding by
ARTS COUNCIL ENGLAND
LOTTERY FUNDED

www.piperkeys.com

Laylah Ali
Comfort, 2018

4 color screenprint
11 × 17 inches
Signed and numbered
Edition of 100

Printed Matter, Inc.

231 11th Avenue
New York NY 10001
T 212 925 0325

www.printedmatter.org

Mon–Wed: 11am–7pm
Thu–Fri: 11am–8pm
Sat: 11am–7pm
Sun: 12pm–6pm

38 St. Mark's Place
New York, NY 10003

Wed–Fri: 2–8pm
Sat: 12–8pm
Sun: 12–6pm

MANIFESTO
PROPOSITION
10

PLYMOUT
COLLEGE O
ART IS A
INDEPENDEN
CREATIV
COLLEGE FO
INDEPENDEN
CREATIV
MINDS

WHAT'S YOU
PROPOSITION

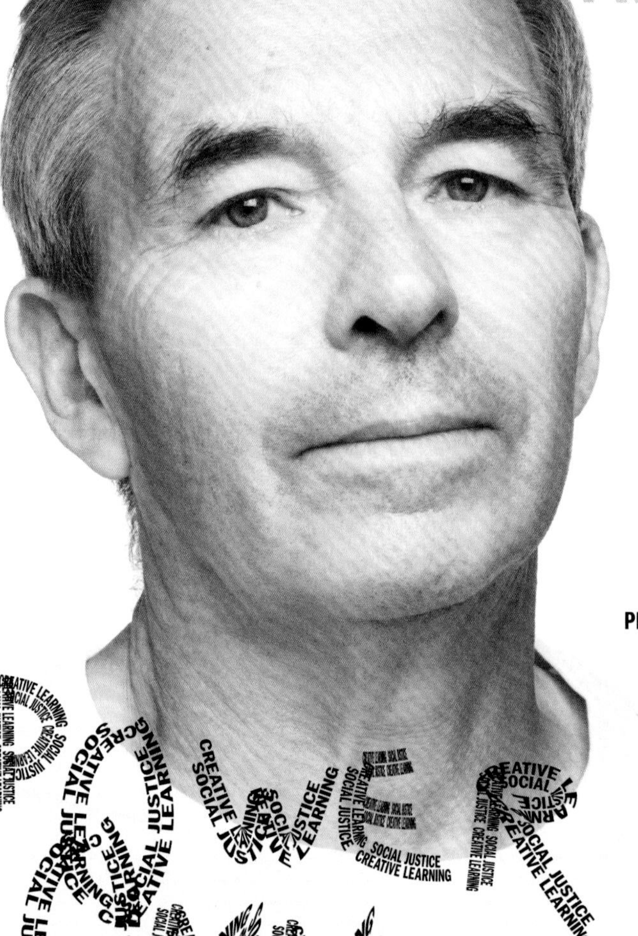

PROPOSITION BY ALAN QUALTROU
MA VISUAL COMMUNICATI

EMPOWER
COMMUNITY

SOCIAL JUSTICE CREATIVE LEARNING

PLYMOUTH
COLLEGE
of ART

OPEN DAYS 20 OCT / 10 NOV / 5 JA
PLYMOUTHART.AC.U

Maeve Rendle

Namely, homely, comely, timely

Live performances and screenings
Thursday 22 November 2018, 6pm
The Whitworth
The University of Manchester
Oxford Road, Manchester, M15 6ER
@WhitworthArt

What cannot be turned aside

Forthcoming solo exhibition
(dates to be announced)
Touchstones Rochdale
The Esplanade, Rochdale, OL16 1AQ
@Touchstones
@ContempForward

Generously supported by Touchstones Rochdale
and the Whitworth with financial support from
the Foyle Foundation, University of Central
Lancashire and Arts Council England using
public funding from the National Lottery